Thumbprint Mysteries

SIGN OF BLOOD

BY

RICHARD FORREST

CB

CONTEMPORARY BOOKS

a division of NTC/CONTEMPORARY PUBLISHING GROUP
Lincolnwood, Illinois USA

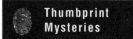

Thumbprint
Mysteries

MORE THUMBPRINT MYSTERIES

by Richard Forrest:

Sign of the Beast
Sign of Terror

This is a work of fiction. The characters, incidents, and dialogues are products of the author's imagination and are not to be construed as real. Any resemblance to actual events or persons, living or dead, is entirely coincidental.

Cover Illustration: Troy Thomas

ISBN: 0-8092-0677-3

Published by Contemporary Books,
a division of NTC/Contemporary Publishing Group, Inc.,
4255 West Touhy Avenue,
Lincolnwood (Chicago), Illinois 60646-1975 U.S.A.

8 9 0 QB 0 9 8 7 6 5 4 3 2 1

CHAPTER 1

Diff James was filled with joy over this new experience.

They were surrounded by white as soon as they dipped into the clouds. The return to open sky gave a feeling of bird-like flight and a view of the world he had never seen before. They flew high above the town of Morgan with its surrounding woods and mountains. A highway cut through the hills that held ant-size cars moving slowly under their winged shadow. He was amazed and thrilled at his first airplane ride.

The twin-engine Piper Aztec banked over Loon Lake, which gave him an eagle's view of the deep blue water. A pine forest embraced lake banks while the mountains beyond cupped the valley with green fingers.

Holly Wilson was strapped into the next seat. The narrow cabin caused their legs and hips to touch, which made her smile. He turned to watch the scenery outside the window in order to ignore her nearness. Neither realized that in four minutes there would be an event that would take a man's life in a way that would haunt their lives.

*   *   *

That morning Holly had knocked on the door of his garage apartment. She hadn't had to come very far since she lived with her father, Police Chief Ray Wilson, in the big house with the wide porch twenty yards down the driveway.

"Wake up, sleepyhead!" she had yelled with another blow on the screen door. "It's a beautiful Saturday and the day is wasting away."

Since Diff could not speak, he couldn't yell back to say he wanted to sleep late this morning. She kept up the pounding until he was forced to tumble from bed and throw on a bathrobe. He picked up the pad he used for notes as he walked through the small apartment. 'I don't have to work today,' he wrote. 'I'm trying to sleep late and will go back to bed if you'll go away.'

She read the note with a tilted smile when he handed it around the edge of the screen door. Early morning sunlight fell across her long hair and turned it a gold-red. She wore a white blouse, tight tan shorts, and snow-white tennis shoes. These were her usual casual clothes, but the sight and nearness of her took his breath away.

She ripped the note and looked at him until their eyes locked. She held the pieces in her palm and let them blow away in the gentle wind. "It's too nice a day to be a slugabed," she said. "I bet we can do something you've never done before."

He shrugged as his way to ask what she meant.

"I bet you've never been up in an airplane," she said.

He nodded to indicate that he probably hadn't, which

she already knew since she knew that many of his childhood memories were lost.

"Well, that's what we're going to do this beautiful day. Mountain Tours has started their summer season. That means sightseeing planes that fly over the forests and mountains around Morgan begin today. We've been invited to be the first passengers. How does that sound to you?"

She took his smile to mean yes. What he could not tell Holly Wilson was that he would go to hell and back for her if she asked. As long as he could not speak and had to communicate with her by hand gestures, shakes of the head, and notes on a pad, he never would tell her his true feelings.

*   *   *

Holly had driven her sky-blue Saturn to the airport and parked in back of the airport office. As they walked past the half dozen small private planes tied down along the edge of the runway, they were met by a large dog who bounded toward them with a fast-wagging tail. He seemed so glad to see Diff that his whole body shook with pleasure.

"Hey, Bushy," Holly said as she patted the large dog. "You've found your friend."

Diff scratched the large dog's ears and again wondered about his breed. Bushy seemed to be part shepherd, part Saint Bernard, with a little Newfoundland thrown in for good measure. He didn't look like any other dog they had ever seen, but the odd mixture made him large and friendly.

The Morgan airport located on the shore of Loon Lake consisted of one concrete runway. A single-story, cement-block building contained the manager's office, radio room, and snack bar. There was one hangar for general repairs and two smaller buildings set in a row next to the runway. A large sign on the first announced, "Mountain

Tours—See the Beautiful Adirondacks by Air." A similar building further down had the same size sign which announced, "Scenic Tours—See It All by Plane." Diff and Holly smiled at the signs since they knew the two groups were archenemies.

There was a small dock on the lake where Mountain Tours usually tied their floatplane. Diff saw that the pontoon plane was not there, which meant that one of the two Mountain Tour pilots was probably ferrying some fishermen to a distant lake. Many of these camps were so remote and far from roads that they could only be reached by air or very long hikes.

Ralph Macon, co-owner of Mountain Tours, had met them by the two-engine Piper Aztec they were flying that day. "You are the first passengers for this year's tour," he had said. "You guys get a free ride, but you pay by hearing me practice my new tourist talk."

"Fine with us, Ralph," Holly had said. "We're looking forward to the trip since Diff has never been up in a plane before."

Ralph smiled. "If I had the other plane today, we might show him a couple of flying tricks. Even so, I'll try to make it interesting."

"I heard you might run flights up from New York City," Holly said.

"That's what we hope to do. We're in the last stages of talks now," Ralph said. "If this new tour business with a tie to the airlines works, I have the feeling that Mead and I are going to make a bundle of money with our little flying service. We'll drive those scumbags of Scenic Tours back under the rocks they crawled out from under."

*   *   *

Ralph turned around in the pilot's seat and waved at Diff and Holly. He cupped a hand over one ear and pointed to the headsets in front of their seats.

They put on their earphones and immediately heard Ralph speaking to them over the intercom. "Can you guys hear okay?" He watched them both nod. "We are now over Morgan at twenty-five hundred feet. How do you like the flight?"

Diff and Holly held up their thumbs. "Great!" Holly yelled loud enough to be heard over the engines.

"I am going to circle over town and then fly across Loon Lake toward Bald Mountain," Ralph said. As soon as he had spoken, the plane banked steeply to the right. Although Holly was securely fastened by the seat belt, the turn threw her against Diff. She felt a small tremor run through her body as she looked at him. Diff was a tall man with broad shoulders and a wide smile. He was in excellent physical shape due to early morning runs that crisscrossed the town and its surroundings.

Diff felt that Holly was only nice to him because she felt sorry for him. He felt her shiver at their closeness because she was repelled by his lack of speech. He gave her top marks for being a good actress. If he didn't know better, he would almost think that she really liked him.

The aircraft banked to the left. Holly was thrown in the other direction, and it was time for Diff's shoulder to press against hers.

I want to run my hands through his hair and down his cheek, she thought. *If I ever did that, he'd be so shocked he would probably never speak to me again.* She almost laughed aloud at that. As far as she knew, Diff had never spoken a word to her or to anyone else.

The plane leveled out over Morgan. They looked out the windows to see the town spread before them. Holly touched his shoulder and pointed. Diff looked where her finger pointed and recognized the Wilson house and garage with his apartment at the rear of the lot. The house sat at the top of a hill on a street that ran down to Court House Square. Main Street was beyond the square, and two blocks down was where the small police headquarters was located.

Morgan was a town of ten thousand in upstate New York, surrounded by the Adirondack Mountains. There was little industry, which meant the town depended on tourism for most of its employment. In summer the area was host to campers, boaters, and hikers. In fall the deer hunters arrived, while winter months brought cross-country and downhill skiers.

It was a pleasant place to live, and for the most part the town was crime free. Ray Wilson's small force of fifteen cops was mostly concerned with traffic duty, school crossings, and teenage problems. The occasional important crime was so rare that it was handled personally by Chief Wilson.

The plane banked as it circled over the town. "We are now flying back toward Loon Lake," Ralph said. He began a rehearsal for the speech he would give when he flew tourists on these trips. "This deep lake is famous throughout New York State for its excellent fishing. Since it is not far from the town of Morgan, part of the ice is cleared of snow in winter. Skating and ice-sail race festivals are often held here. In the distance beyond the lake you can see Bald Mountain. That area is known for its bears and other examples of wildlife."

Diff was in love with flying. The first minutes of this trip were enough to prove that to him. There were now three things that he wanted more than anything else in life. He mentally listed them in proper order: first, he wanted Holly to love him; after that he wanted to join the police force. Such a job not only would be interesting, but would give him the income to support Holly and take flying lessons, the third item on his list.

It hit him with a sharp punch of depression that he could do none of these things. He could not speak, so he could not join the police force. A great deal of police work required asking people questions and using car radios and walkie-talkies. Flying an airplane required the use of a radio to communicate with the control tower. But without a voice, joining the police force, flying a plane, and claiming Holly were all impossible.

"Hey," the pilot yelled over the microphone. "Look at that plane down below us. It looks like Mead. My partner has taken the floatplane out for a test flight."

Ralph Macon banked the plane to give them a better view. In the distance below them and directly over the center of the lake was a bright-red, single-engine plane with pontoons for water landings.

"Look at that baby go," Ralph Macon said. "Hey, what's going on?" His voice had an edge of alarm. "He's in trouble!"

Diff and Holly watched in horror as a thin trail of black smoke came out of the floatplane's engine. The bright-colored craft seemed to be fighting to keep on a straight course across the lake. The unstable wobble of its wings showed that it was a losing battle.

"He's really in trouble!" Ralph yelled. "He's in deep—" Because Holly was in the cabin he did not complete the sentence.

The floatplane went into a steep dive aimed at the surface of the lake. The thin trail of black smoke from its engine streaked back over the plane like an angry tail.

"He's going to crash!" Holly yelled in alarm.

The pilot of the plane below them seemed to be trying to regain control. The floatplane's wings rocked back and forth as it dipped toward the water. For a few moments it seemed to recover as the nose turned up and then it dove again.

The plane could not return to level flight. Inexperienced as he was, Diff realized the red plane was in a death dive. He also knew that a rescue attempt would have to be made.

Loon Lake was large for the area, but from their height he could still see both shores. He looked away from the troubled aircraft below to see the peak of Bald Mountain directly ahead. He estimated that the floatplane was in line with the top of Bald Mountain.

When he looked back toward their rear, he saw the far end of Loon Lake and the small dock where the floatplane docked. The mountaintop and dock were in a line with the airplane that was now spitting large spurts of smoke from its engine. Diff had the crashing plane exactly located.

"She's going down!" Ralph yelled.

They watched the floatplane take one last dip over the water before it made a final plunge. It hit and dove below the surface.

"Stall! Stall! Stall!" an automatic voice warned. Their plane seemed to hang in the air a moment before it nosed over and spun toward the water.

Although this was his first airplane ride, Diff had read about planes. He knew that aircraft were kept in the air by the movement of air over the wings. Any plane, depending on its size, wingspan, and weight, had to move at a certain speed to keep this air movement strong enough to hold the plane up. If a plane fell below that speed, it went into a stall. A stalled aircraft did not fly but fell out of the air.

That was what was happening to them at this moment. The plane had gone into a spin that their pilot fought to control.

Holly fearfully clutched Diff's arm.

Ralph Macon increased speed and pushed the nose down until the plane's engines began to chew the air again. The pilot regained control of the craft at the last moment, and they zoomed across the water a dozen feet above the surface.

"Mayday! Mayday! Morgan airport!" Ralph shouted into the radio mike. "This is Mountain Tour Two. Do you read me? . . . There is a Mayday of Mountain Tour One. She's gone down in Loon Lake. . . . I don't know where. She crashed in the water somewhere. Get help!"

Maybe Ralph didn't know where the plane had gone down, but Diff James did.

CHAPTER 2

Senior police officers standing on the shore of Loon Lake looked like matched bookends. Ray Wilson, police chief for the town of Morgan, was a huge man over six feet tall and closer to three than two hundred pounds. At his side was County Sheriff Big Red Downs. Both men were of equal size, but Big Red wore a wide-brimmed hat, which made him appear larger.

The shore of Loon Lake near the Mountain Tour pier and the Morgan Airport was a hive of activity. Two town police cars were parked near the dock with the volunteer ambulance alongside. The medics sat in the rear of their van playing cards. Sheriff's department cars and a pickup from the airport were neatly tucked into the line. Curious townspeople had driven over to watch, but they were kept at a distance by a police barricade.

Morgan's city limits ran down the center of the lake. Exactly where the crashed airplane was found would determine who had charge of the investigation. If the plane was closer to this shore, the Morgan police department would be in charge. If the plane crash site was nearer the far side of the lake, it would be in the county and a matter to be handled by the sheriff's department. Federal crash investigators would look into the accident no matter where the plane was found.

Sergeant Ned Toms of the Morgan police was in charge of the area rescue team. His crew was unloading diving equipment from their truck. Team members were men and women of great skill in different areas. Some of the group were trained mountain climbers who could rescue climbers, hikers, and skiers. There were also SCUBA divers trained for water recoveries. Other men and women were trained in opening crushed cars, fixing dangerous electrical lines, and other areas such as wild animal control. Diff James belonged to several rescue group sections.

Toms and his other divers began to climb into wet suits and check their SCUBA gear. A large rubber Zodiac raft, with a hundred-horsepower outboard motor mounted on its stern, waited at the small dock.

Diff and Holly climbed out of the Piper after it landed and walked across the runway toward the lakeshore. Ray Wilson turned to wave at his daughter. "You saw exactly where it went down?" he asked when they arrived.

Diff pointed to the top of Bald Mountain and brought his arm down across the water to stop with his finger pointed at the small dock.

"Diff says the crash was near the center of the lake on a direct line between the mountain and this dock," Holly said. "It ought to be easy to find."

"Don't know about that," Sheriff Downs said. "There

are parts of Loon Lake where we don't know how deep it goes."

Sergeant Toms adjusted the air tank on his back and put a face mask over his forehead. "That's true," Toms said. "We know some places are over a hundred feet deep."

"Can you dive to the bottom?" Ray asked.

"I believe so, Chief. If we watch to make sure we don't come up too fast, we can go down to a hundred feet. We'll take powerful lanterns with us."

"When the floatplane went down, it dove directly into the water," Holly said. "Whoever the pilot was didn't get out. Or at least we didn't see anyone get out."

Ralph Macon drove up in a jeep. "The only person authorized to fly that craft was my partner, Mead Acorn. He must be the one who went down in her. I've already called his wife and she's on her way."

Diff climbed into the Zodiac and pulled the cord to start the hundred-horsepower outboard. Rescue-team divers climbed aboard and were soon busy with each man checking the equipment of the man in front of him.

Diff briefly closed his eyes to recall the sight picture he had of Bald Mountain from the airplane. He opened his eyes to steer the Zodiac directly into the center of the lake on a line that ran from Bald Mountain to the Mountain Tours pier. When they neared the spot where he estimated the plane went in, he cut the engine and let the Zodiac drift in a circle.

"This it?" Toms asked.

Diff nodded.

"Gotcha," the police sergeant said. He held up a thumb, pulled down his face mask, and put the air regulator in his mouth. He gave another thumbs-up sign before he tumbled backwards over the side of the boat.

The other divers followed and sank quickly out of sight.

It was a technicolor day. Bright sunlight bounced off white clouds while the image of Bald Mountain was reflected in the clear lake water.

It was half an hour before Toms surfaced, pulled up his mask, and took the regulator out of his mouth. "Are you sure this is the spot?" he yelled at Diff.

Diff nodded his head to indicate that it was.

"There's nothing down there. Water is clear and I estimate depth at seventy feet along here. A plane is a pretty big thing, you know, but I don't see her."

The other divers surfaced in a semicircle around the boat. Toms divided them into two teams. He would lead one group in a search back toward the pier while the other divers worked a line toward the far shore on the Bald Mountain side.

Meanwhile, Holly drove her Saturn back toward the small airport building to get coffee for the police and rescue workers. During the short drive she found, as she did so often, that she thought of Diff.

Diff had wandered barefoot into Morgan at dawn ten years ago. He had been nearly starved, dazed, and confused. A passing cab driver had tried to talk with him and had radioed for police help. Ray Wilson had been the first cop to arrive. When he had tried to speak with Diff, he realized that not only was the young man confused, he was also hungry and could not speak.

In that first year Holly's father had tried very hard to find out who Diff was and where he had come from. Diff was not much help with the search since he could not speak and had few memories. The memories he did have came in bad dreams that haunted his sleep.

In the following years Ray and Holly had helped Diff

start a new life. He lived in the small apartment over their garage and learned to read and write while he worked as a janitor at police headquarters.

It wasn't until last winter that Diff discovered he had originally come from the town of Waycross only thirty miles away. They had finally located his mentally ill father, who was now a patient in a nursing home. This abusive father had locked Diff in a hidden room for several years. This action along with other forms of isolation and abuse had taken his voice and most of his early memories.

Holly parked by the side of the building. The small snack bar was empty of customers and also the lone employee who usually ran it. She put her hand on the side of the tall coffee urn and felt that it was still warm. She would pour a dozen coffees and carry them back to the lake in a large box. The chief would settle payment with the airport later today. She went behind the counter and began to fill styrofoam cups with coffee.

She was putting the lids on when she heard voices in the next room. "Oh, darling," the woman said, "I've missed you so."

"You shouldn't be with me," the man said. "Someone might see us together when you should be out at the lake."

"He's been acting so strange recently that I think he knows."

"About us?" the man asked. Holly recognized the voice of Gary Towns, the airport manager. "You know, with the temper he has, he might come after me with a gun."

"I couldn't help it," she said. "I think he might have followed me last Thursday when we met at your place. I think he knows all about us, Gary."

"Oh, great. That's really great."

"Maybe the plane did crash and he was . . ."

"No such luck. Mead is too good a pilot. That guy Diff had it wrong, that's all. No way would Mead crash into the water like that. He'd make a recovery and land on the lake."

"I love you, Gary," the woman's voice said, and Holly knew she was listening to Mary Acorn, the floatplane pilot's wife. "There's more. I told Mead I wanted a divorce."

"What did he say?"

"He laughed and said he would fight me in court. He swore I'd walk away from the marriage without a penny. He asked if I knew you had money troubles because of all the new equipment you bought."

"He'll hang on to every penny," Gary said. "There is no one in the world more stubborn than Mead."

Holly cleared her throat as she filled a box with cups. She hated to accidentally overhear people's private problems. She stepped back from the coffee urn and around the corner of the small snack bar so they would see and hear her.

"Who the hell is that?" Gary said as he stormed out of his office. "Oh, it's you, Holly. How long have you been here?"

"I'm sorry, Gary, I didn't mean to eavesdrop." Gary wore a leather flying jacket with an air force officer's hat tilted on his forehead. His usual wide grin was now replaced by a worried frown. Mary Acorn had a hand to her cheek in surprise. She was a silver blond with an hourglass figure and deep blue eyes. *They are an attractive couple*, Holly thought. *Too bad she is married to someone else.*

"I'm taking coffee out to the police and rescue crews," Holly said. "We'll settle up later."

"Okay, sure, fine," Gary said with an impatient wave of his hand. "Forget paying. Consider this my gift to the rescue operation."

"Thanks," Holly said as she left carrying the carton filled with cups of coffee. "I'll tell everyone about the free coffee."

He stared angrily at her. "Well, there's not much I can do about what you heard, is there? Please try and keep it to yourself."

*   *   *

The sheriff and police chief watched the SCUBA divers come out of the water. The swimmers walked awkwardly up the beach in their rubber flippers and removed their masks. Sergeant Toms shook his head. "We looked where Diff said, Chief. There's nothing all the way to the shore on this side of the lake."

They looked across the lake to see other divers on the far shore. The lead diver signaled with a wave of his arms.

"That's a 'not found' on the far side of the lake too," Sergeant Toms said. "That plane is not where Diff said it was. I'd stake my life on that, Chief."

"Well, you know how wrong a witness can be in all that excitement," Big Red said. "The guy had his first airplane ride and thought he saw another plane going into the drink. No wonder he made a mistake."

"We'll try boats with dragging hooks on either side of the center line," Ray said.

"That's a faster way to do it, Chief," Big Red said. "We aren't going to hurt no one if we do find it. If it's there, it's been down too long for anyone to live. What do you think about radar?"

"What kind of radar?" Ray asked.

"I was thinking fish radar might show something as

large as an airplane. I got one mounted in my cruiser docked over at Wright's boat landing."

"Wouldn't hurt to try," Ray said. "I'd sure like to find that plane." As Big Red drove over to the other boat landing, Ray gave orders for the rescue team to shuck their wet suits and air tanks and get boats to continue the search.

A red pickup truck screeched to a halt behind the line of rescue cars and trucks and turned in a half circle, which threw up a cloud of dirt and sand. The truck held a gun rack at the rear of the cab with empty cases of beer filling the bed of the truck. The two men inside were large and red-faced, wearing dirty T-shirts and overalls.

Holly and Diff, who were passing out coffee to members of the rescue teams, scowled at the new arrivals. "Look who just drove up," Holly said. "Our favorite good old country boys, the Laman brothers."

Luke and Joe Laman were talking to the card-playing members of the volunteer ambulance crew. After a few minutes they gave huge hoots of laughter and walked over to Diff and Holly.

"Hey, Retard," Luke Laman said. "You go in big bird up in sky, huh?"

The Lamans laughed.

"See other big bird go down, down, down," Joe Laman said. "Other big bird go splash in water. Is that what you told Ray Wilson, Retard?"

"He didn't tell Ray nothing," Luke said, "because Retard here can't talk."

"Cat got your tongue, Dummy?" Joe said as both men gave more hoots of laughter at their old joke.

Diff clenched his fists and started for the two men.

"Hey, lookee here," Luke said. "Dummy wants to play."

"Let's teach old Retard a lesson," Joe said.

"With pleasure, " Luke replied.

"No way," Holly said as she stepped between them. She put her arms around Diff. "They aren't worth it. Believe me, they really aren't worth it."

"Dummy Retard hides behind a woman," Luke said.

Diff tried to step around Holly but she only held him tighter. Ray Wilson saw what was happening and hurried over. "Okay, you guys, break it up. Do all of you hear me? Any trouble here and you all bunk in a cell tonight. Luke and Joe, get back in your truck and get out of here. Diff, go out on the dock and find out how the search is going."

"We ain't done nothing," Luke Laman said. "And if there was going to be any fight here, old Retard there was going to start it. We were minding our own business and came to find out what help you needed in the search."

"We have things under control, boys. So run on over to the Morgan Bar and play the pinball machine like you usually do," Ray said. "You heard me."

Holly dragged Diff toward the dock. "Did you know that the airport manager and Mead Acorn's wife are having an affair?"

Diff shook his head.

"That would just be a bit of juicy gossip if there wasn't something very funny going on around here today." They stood at the end of the dock and watched rowboats slowly crisscross the lake. "You've got to learn to stay away from those Laman brothers, Diff. They want to make trouble and start a fight. But remember, they always go around in pairs so it will be two of them against you."

The sheriff's motorboat was cruising a back-and-forth pattern across the lake. Several rowboats held standing men who pushed long poles with hooks deep into the water. They were making a careful search pattern of squares that would eventually cover the whole lake area.

Ralph Macon joined them on the dock. "You know," he said, "several people saw the floatplane take off early this morning. It can't stay up this long even with a full gas tank." They quietly looked out over the water as the sun began to dip behind Bald Mountain. The last light of day spilled over the hills and streaked along the water. The boats on the water finished their search pattern and began to row toward shore.

"I think they're done," Ralph said.

"They haven't found anything," Holly added.

"I don't think there's anything there to find," Ralph said.

"You saw it go down too," Holly said.

"Not really," Ralph said. "I saw that he was in trouble, but then I was too busy flying my plane. I had to take your word for it when you say it went down in the water. I think he crashed on the other side of Bald Mountain, and we might not find the wreck for months."

The police chief walked slowly out to the end of the dock as the sheriff's boat came alongside. Big Red shook his head. "We've wasted a lot of man-hours out here today for nothing," he said as Diff grabbed his line and tied the boat. "Do you know what this is going to cost my department in overtime?"

"Damn it all, Red," Ray said. "We're talking about a man's life out there."

The huge sheriff shook his head. "Sorry. We've searched every inch of Loon Lake and there's no floatplane in that water. You hear me, Mr. Diff? There is no plane in that water."

"But we saw it," Holly said. "Diff took careful sightings to help the search."

"Well, he was wrong," the sheriff said. "I promise you that there is no airplane in that lake."

"I'm afraid he's right," Ray said. "It was a good search and they didn't turn up anything."

Diff and Holly looked at each other with a glance that said they both knew what they had seen, but there was no way to prove it. They had seen an airplane crash and disappear as surely as if it had never existed.

Chapter 3

"Good morning, Mr. James," Sally Way, the police station clerk, said with a cat-like smile.

Diff smiled back at the attractive blond who seemed stuffed into a uniform two sizes too small. She leaned across the desk to speak in a soft voice. "The chief says you have to sign in when you come into the building," she said as she pushed a pad toward him.

Diff was puzzled, since he worked here. His job took him in and out of the building a dozen times a day. Certainly Ray did not mean for him to sign the book each time he came in or went outside.

"Don't look at me, Diff—these are orders from the top. And you know me, I am only to follow and obey. Give me the word, hon, and I'm yours to obey." She smiled again and leaned closer.

Diff blushed as hurried down the hall to Ray's office.

Sally looked after him with her feline smile still on her

face. The telephone board blinked and she snatched up the receiver. "Morgan Police Department," she snapped. One way or the other, she was going to get Diff to ask her out. Maybe he would have to write stuff out on a pad. But that was okay with her because he was a real hunk that she wanted a piece of.

"I said 'Morgan Police,'" she said abruptly. ". . . No, we don't get kittens down from trees anymore. . . . We stopped doing cats last year when an officer fell out of an apple tree and broke his arm after the tabby barfed a hairball over him. Try the volunteer ambulance, since I happen to know they love cats."

She hung up with a crooked grin. *There's more than one way to skin a cat*, she thought. *That little phone call will teach Roy Jenkins, the ambulance driver, not to stand up Sally Way.*

*   *   *

Police Chief Ray Wilson stood at the window of his office with feet apart and hands clasped behind his back. "I wonder what they're arguing about," he said in a voice nearly to himself.

Diff came in to stand by his side and look out the window at Mary Acorn. The wife of the co-owner of Mountain Tours was talking in the parking lot with airport manager Gary Towns. They were too far away to hear their words, but they looked like they were in a heated argument.

"Holly told me about those two," Ray said. "It's very interesting since Mary's husband seems to be missing and perhaps dead."

Mary Acorn walked away from Gary and marched angrily toward the door of the police building.

"Perhaps we'll find out what the lovebirds were fighting about," Ray said as he picked up the phone. "Thanks, Sally. Send Mrs. Acorn right in. . . . I told you before, Sally.

Since he works here, Diff does not have to sign in and out." He hung up with a tired sigh. "Oh, well." He went to open the door for Mary Acorn. "Stay here, Diff," he said. "I want you to hear what she has to say."

"My husband is missing!" Mary Acorn said before she was fully in the office. "I demand to know what you are doing about it!"

Ray sat behind his desk and tented his fingers in an attempt to look dignified. Diff sat quietly on the corner of the couch. "You saw our lake search, Mrs. Acorn. Without another lead I don't know what else this department can do."

"I demand action!" she yelled.

"We have searched Loon Lake due to a report that someone saw your husband's plane go down. As you know, we did not find it in the lake. A few local private pilots are making an air search of the whole county."

"What else are you doing?"

"Nothing."

"You will be impeached for this!" she shouted.

"I do not believe that police chiefs are impeached. We are fired by our grateful public."

"I will have the mayor fire you!"

"He does that almost weekly," Ray said. His tone changed to a strong, official one. "Let me tell you something, Mrs. Acorn. We have no evidence of foul play as far as your husband is concerned."

"He is missing!"

"That may be. If someone would report that to me officially, I could put out an all-points bulletin to the whole state."

"Well, he's gone."

"Has he been missing for more than twenty-four hours?"

"Yes. It's been more than two days now. I don't know where he is."

"Then I suggest you file a missing persons report with us. We will then start a statewide search for him. Go see Miss Way at the front desk. She will give you the right forms and find a place for you to fill them out. That will start things going, and I assure you we will do our very best."

"Well, if that's the way it's done."

"It is," Ray answered. "Do you have any idea what might have happened to your husband?"

"Well, he and his partner, Ralph Macon, are very close to a contract with one of the major airlines for some feeder service to Morgan. If they get the contract, it will mean a lot of money. That will make some people very unhappy."

"Who would that be?" Ray asked.

"The people who own Scenic. They do the same thing as Mountain Tours and would be mad as hell. They'd do anything to stop that contract because it would ruin them."

"I'll look into that," Ray said. "By the way, I saw you in the parking lot talking to Gary Towns. You seemed to be having quite an argument. Care to tell me if it was about your husband?"

"We were talking about another personal matter that has nothing to do with my missing husband."

"Isn't that interesting?" Ray said after she left. "She's having an affair with Gary, and her husband has disappeared."

Diff wondered about that and also about the interesting fact that Gary was an experienced flyer. This case seemed to be all tied up with airplanes and people who knew how to fly.

*   *   *

Holly burst through the front door of the police station and hurried toward her father's office. She almost fell over the waist-high door that led to the rear hall when it wouldn't swing open. She looked at Sally, who sat at the communications desk staring down at the sign-in sheets and pretending not to notice Holly.

"I almost killed myself on this gate," Holly said. "It's never been locked before."

"That was before we had sign-in. No one comes in without signing the book," Sally said as she ignored Holly. She looked at her nails before she began to pick at one of her fingers.

"Hey, come on, Sally," Holly said. "I'm here to see my dad. Open the door."

"Everyone signs; that is the chief's order," Sally said without looking at Holly.

"Sally, you and I went to grade school, middle school, and high school together. You have known me all your life."

"Everyone signs the book."

"All right," Holly said as she grabbed the sheet and scrawled her name. "Now let me in."

For the first time the two women's eyes met. "You know," Sally said, "there's lots of talk around town about you and that guy who can't speak."

"That guy who can't talk has a name, Sally. You not only know it, but you see him ten times a day, since he works here."

"I have never noticed him. Anyway, we don't think it's a good idea for you to be seeing so much of that man since he lives almost in your home. It's going to give you a bad name."

Holly's mouth dropped open. "What are you talking about?"

"You could get in trouble taking advantage of a retarded person you are supposed to be teaching."

"You are nuts!" Holly said as she hurried toward the chief's office.

Ray's door burst open when Mary Acorn rushed out. "Where do I get a missing persons form?" she snapped.

"Front desk," Holly said.

Mary grabbed Holly's arm. "Hey, thanks a lot for spilling the beans. You are a real friend."

"What are you talking about?"

"I think your dad suspects something about Gary and me. And if he does, he could use it against us," Mary said.

Holly had no reply, since she had told her father and Diff about what she had overheard in the airport snack bar.

"Just thanks loads, big mouth," Mary said as she dropped Holly's arm and hurried down the hall.

Boy, am I popular this morning, Holly thought as she opened the door to Ray's office.

* * *

It was barbecue swim-party time in the Wilsons' backyard. This party was a yearly affair that took place at the beginning of each summer. Ray presided over the barbecue with the same authority he showed at police headquarters. He stood over the fire, flipping steaks and hamburgers, wearing a high chef's hat and a long white apron that came down to his ankles. Big red letters on the apron said, "We are the good guys."

The complete Morgan police force, less two men and one woman cop on duty, were all present, wearing bright shorts or swimsuits. Diff also wore his swim trunks and sat at one side of the pool on a lawn chair. He watched Holly climb the diving board in her bright yellow one-piece bathing suit which set off her trim legs and red-gold hair. She stood on the end of the diving board and bounced a few times to get ready for her dive. The sight of her nearly caused him to bite his fingers holding a hot dog.

While Diff watched Holly, Sally watched Diff. The police clerk wore a black string bikini that was the smallest allowed by law. Her hip-swaying walk across the patio attracted every male's glance except for Diff's, which was focused on the diving board as he waited for Holly to make her dive.

Mary Acorn and Gary Towns stood behind Diff, looking over the party. "Look at that fancy swimming pool," Mary sneered to Gary in a low voice.

"And the barbecue, and the fancy patio, much less all that food he's cooking. It must have cost a fortune," Gary said to her in a still lower voice.

"And he's supposed to have all this on a small-town police chief's salary? Fat chance!" Mary said.

"He's on the take somewhere," Gary agreed. "He's got mucho bucks coming in from somewhere to support a life like this."

Diff burned in anger and considered throwing Gary along with his leather flying jacket into the pool. Anyone who dressed like that in the middle of a hot afternoon needed to go into the pool. Diff knew how Chief Ray Wilson could afford this fancy patio and pool. Diff, in gratitude for what Ray had done for him, had dug the pool by hand, poured the concrete, and laid the patio. It had taken hundreds of hours of back-breaking work to create what looked like an expensive purchase.

"If the chief's on the take, we could pay him off with some of Mead's insurance money—make him stop this investigation," Mary said to Gary in a whisper that could be heard by Diff's acute ears. Since he could not speak,

Diff knew that people often considered him retarded. They would often say things in front of him that they would not usually say.

"Look at the size of that man and this place," Gary said. "He'd want every nickel you're going to get."

"Maybe you're right—we better forget a payoff."

This was information that Ray would like to have, Diff thought. Later when he had a chance, he'd write a long note to Ray and tell him exactly what he had just heard. These two lovers were spending life insurance money for a man that no one knew was dead.

Holly made a perfect swan dive into the water, which made everyone clap except for a frowning Sally, who sat next to Diff.

"I know you live in that garage apartment over there," Sally said. "How about showing me around your place? I bet if we tried, we could turn up something really interesting to do alone."

Holly heaved herself from the pool and deliberately shook herself so that water sprayed over Sally. "Here's for interesting," she said.

"Hey, watch it!" Sally said.

"Oh, sorry," Holly answered.

Ray waved a fork and called across the patio to Diff. "Take over the cooking for a couple of minutes, will you?"

Diff took the fork from Ray and flipped a couple of hamburgers while Ray spoke with Mary Acorn. He noticed that as soon as Ray approached her, Gary moved to the far side of the pool.

"Thank you for stopping by, Mrs. Acorn. I wanted to let you know that we are doing everything we can to find your husband," Ray said.

"It doesn't seem to be enough," she said. "He's still

gone and there's no word from him."

"I have told my force, the sheriff's department, and the forest rangers to look for his airplane. We have also sent an APB to six states. That's an all-points bulletin to all police agencies in the area. There's not much else we can do without some sort of lead. Do you have any idea why he would leave?"

"No, I have no idea. In fact, when Ralph signs this new airline contract in New York, Mountain Tours is really going to make money. Mead had every reason to stay."

"At my expense!" Harry Black said. "Your husband was going to take money out of my pocket!" The new arrival was the owner of Scenic Tours, Mountain Tour's rival and enemy. He was a thin, nervous man who always seemed jumpy.

"Calm down, Harry," Ray said.

"I can't be calm when I think about what Mead Acorn is doing to me," Harry said as his hands chopped the air. "That guy is out to ruin me. He's taking the airline contract away from us to drive me out of business."

"It's called fair competition," Mary said. "Mead was just smarter than you."

"If I could get my hands on him, I'd rip his smart head off."

"There will be none of that, Harry," Ray said. "I don't want to hear any more of that talk."

Sheriff Red Downs parked his cruiser behind Harry Black's car and walked toward Ray. "I heard what you said. No one can hurt Mead Acorn now," he said.

"All right, I'll pipe down about hurting him, but it doesn't stop me from thinking it," Harry said.

"Maybe we'd like to hear more about your feelings concerning Mead Acorn," the sheriff said.

"What are you talking about?" Harry asked.

"We've found the airplane with Mead's body in it."

"Where?" Ray snapped.

"My husband . . . dead?" Mary said as she slumped into a chair.

"I didn't realize his wife was here," the sheriff said.

"Where was the plane found?" Ray repeated.

"Where? I'll tell you where," the sheriff said. "We found it exactly where Diff said it would be. Except that it was not under the lake but floating nice as you please on the surface."

"And the pilot?" Ray asked.

"In the cabin, dead. I can personally identify him as Mead Acorn."

"That's impossible," Ray said. "You were with us the other day when we searched the whole lake. You were the one who swore there was no airplane in that water."

"Maybe there wasn't one *in* the water, but right now there is a seaplane *on* the water. A pontoon plane with Mountain Tours written all over it in big letters is floating on Loon Lake," the sheriff said.

"Wait a minute," Ray said. "You're telling me that Diff and Holly saw a plane go into the water two days ago, a plane we couldn't find, and that same plane is now floating on the lake with a dead pilot?"

"That's exactly what I'm saying, Chief," the sheriff said. "We don't know if he died in the town of Morgan or in the county, so for the time being we both have a murder on our hands."

CHAPTER 4

Ray Wilson stopped his
police cruiser behind Sheriff Downs's car on the shore of
Loon Lake near the Mountain Tour's dock. In the line
along the shore stood the two police officers, Diff, and
Holly, along with several bystanders.

"I thought you said it was located exactly where Diff
saw it go down," Ray said.

"It was," the sheriff said. "But we didn't anchor it like
we should have. It floated toward the left bank. See it
over there?"

Everyone near the dock could clearly see the calmly
floating craft. The bright-red floatplane with "Mountain
Tours" written in large letters on its side was clearly
visible near the far shore.

A gentle breeze from the west had pushed the
airplane across the surface of the water. It came to a
stop at the far side when its pontoons caught in the

rocks that dotted the shallows.

A large moose with her young calf stood in water up to its knees. The animals bent to munch tender grass shoots that grew just under the surface. From time to time the largest of the animals raised her head and looked at the nearby airplane with dull curiosity. The smaller moose seemed to assume that airplanes were common and paid it no attention.

A serious man wearing a dark suit parked his car near the police cruisers. Lars Sikes, the assistant medical examiner for the area, carried a small black medical bag as he walked toward them with a scowl on his face.

"Whose case is this?" the doctor asked gruffly.

"Take a pick, Doc," Ray said. "We don't know where it happened."

Diff pulled the rubber Zodiac raft into the water and began to prime the outboard motor. Holly stood on the dock, ready to cast off the line. Diff held up his right hand with a thumbs-up signal.

"Okay, people," Ray said. "Let's go see what's in that airplane." He stepped into the raft.

"I've already been out there," Sheriff Downs said. "You are about to see something that will blow your minds."

"Won't be anything new to me. I've seen it all," the doctor said as he stepped carefully into the boat. "Let's get this over with."

Diff put the outboard in gear as Holly cast the line to her father who coiled it in the bottom of the Zodiac. They sped across the lake toward the red airplane floating near the lunching moose.

Diff was careful to approach at an angle to the large animal standing in the water. He knew very well that moose could be dangerous. In recent years, the large beasts had emigrated down from Canada and were beginning to populate the woods in upstate New York. They were huge, fearless animals that were willing to fight anything they considered a threat. These lumbering animals often battled cars for highway right-of-way and won. Several automobiles in the Morgan area had recently been totaled. The moose-auto battles had the score of moose four, cars two.

As Diff steered a careful course to the side of the airplane, the moose completed its tender-grass meal and began to walk up the bank into the woods. The calf continued eating until he realized his mother had left and quickly ran after her.

"Glad she decided to leave," the sheriff said as he holstered his pistol. "Hate to have to shoot an animal like that, but we have a crime to look at."

Diff cut the motor and let the Zodiac drift to the side of the plane. He jumped to a pontoon and tied the Zodiac to a wing strut.

"Take a careful look," the sheriff said, "because you guys are not going to believe what you are about to see."

"There's nothing you can show me that will be a surprise," the doctor said with a snort as he pulled himself up to peer in the cabin. He looked for a moment, pulled glasses from his jacket pocket, and looked again. "I'll be damned," he finally said. "I don't believe what I'm seeing. Whoever wrote this did it in blood. Did you or any of your men touch the body, Sheriff?"

"Never opened the door to do that. One look in the window was enough to tell me he was dead. That red writing clinched it," the sheriff said. "Another thing, look at the front of the plane where the engine is supposed to be."

"It looks like it's been torn loose," Ray said. "This airplane looks like it crashed nose-down."

"Exactly," the sheriff said as Ray and Diff looked into the plane cabin. A single word written in blood was on the inside of the cabin-door window. The crooked letters spelled "Revenge." Mead Acorn was slumped over with his head resting against the instruments. The inside of the airplane was filled with water. Algae floated near the ceiling while fish swam around the dead man's legs.

When the doctor pulled open the door, water rushed out and poured over him. Lars mumbled angrily and wrung out his jacket before he bent over to examine the man at the controls. "The body seems to have been pretty well knocked around during the crash," the medical examiner said. "I'll check, but my first guess would be to say that death was caused by the crash."

"Well then," Ray said. "In that case we might not have a murder here after all. We have an ordinary plane crash that the Feds will check out."

"What we have are questions," the sheriff said. "We had a sighting of an airplane crash that we couldn't find. Two days later the same plane appears after it mysteriously bobs to the surface. In that plane we find a pilot who either drowned or was killed in the crash. This ghost plane now has the word 'Revenge' written in blood on a window. I say we have a hell of a lot of questions and no answers."

"Hold your horses," the medical examiner snapped. "I've found something that changes things."

"Would you be so kind as to tell us what that is, or are we going to play twenty questions?" the sheriff asked.

"You don't have to get snippy," the doctor said. "You know, all I am required to do at this point is say that this guy is dead. Everything else can wait until I get him on the table to open him up for my full report."

"Sorry, Doc," the sheriff said. "We're all on edge and I don't like what's going on here. What do you see?"

"Come up here and I'll show you," the medical examiner said.

The plane tilted when the two huge police officers climbed up on the wing so they could see into the small cabin. The medical examiner had pulled back the body in the pilot's seat.

"Looks like a bullet hole," Ray said after he looked at the back of the dead man's head.

"That it is," the doctor said. "There's no drowning here because this man was dead before the plane hit the water. This is murder."

"Wait a sec," Ray said. "Would that shot have killed him right away?"

"No question about that," the doctor said. "A bullet in that part of the body would kill him at once."

The sheriff jumped from the wing into the Zodiac. His heavy weight caused the boat to tip so far that Diff had to throw himself in the opposite direction to keep it from turning over.

Sheriff Downs sat in the bow of the boat and folded his arms in disgust. "We seem to have a dead man who flew an airplane into Loon Lake and disappeared. Somehow it came to the surface two days later. How did he fly that plane? How did it take off when the pilot had a bullet in him? Or if he was shot while in the air, what happened to the killer? How did the murderer get out of the cabin after the crash?"

"I think he was killed on the ground and flown here," Ray said as he climbed into the boat. "Let her rip, Diff. I want to get things moving on this case right away."

Diff put the outboard in gear, turned the rudder for a left turn, and sped away from the plane. The men in the Zodiac were silent during the short trip back to the pier.

The sign of blood, the red "Revenge" written on the cabin window, haunted them.

The Zodiac was tied at the pier and they were climbing into their cars when they remembered that they'd left the doctor on the airplane.

"Oh, boy, Old Lars is never in good humor at best," Sheriff Downs said. "That's going to be one mad doctor."

*   *   *

The confession to the murder of Mead Acorn came at three o'clock that afternoon.

"Sign the book," Sally Way sitting at the front desk of police headquarters said. "Everyone's got to sign the book and state their business."

"My name is Henry Watson," the small man said as he signed his name. Sally wondered if the short man in front of her weighed a hundred and twenty pounds soaking wet. She knew him by sight because he was the teller at the Morgan Bank who cashed her paycheck every week. She knew he was married to Doris Watson, who had the 7-Eleven store out on Route 40. Sally knew right away that married or not, Henry was not a hunk. Therefore, she dismissed him as a possible candidate for anything.

"State your business and who you want to see," Sally said without looking up as her thoughts turned to Diff. Even if he couldn't speak, he was a great-looking guy with a sweet manner.

"Like I said, my name is Henry Watson. I have come to confess to the murder of Mead Acorn."

Sally yawned. "Okay, sure. Have a seat and I'll call the chief, since he takes all confessions. . . ." It suddenly dawned on her what this man had just said. She pressed the red emergency button hidden under the lip of her desk.

Within seconds a police car screeched to a halt in front

of the station. Sergeant Toms, who was writing a shift report in the back room, ran toward the front desk with gun in hand. Ray Wilson's office door slammed against the wall as he ran down the hall pulling his service revolver from its holster. Sally reached into her middle desk drawer and pulled out a .38.

Henry sat on the small leather couch in the waiting area and crossed his legs. He seemed prepared to wait patiently and did not seem surprised when he was quickly surrounded by armed police. On one side the cop from the cruiser stood in the front doorway with a shotgun, while Sally aimed her .38 with both hands. Toms and Ray surrounded the couch from the other side.

"Anything wrong, fellas?" Henry asked in a low voice. "If you guys are busy, I can come back another time."

"Stand up!" Ray ordered. "Get up against the wall with your feet apart and your hands overhead. Pat him down," he said to the other cops without taking his eyes off Henry.

"I don't mean to make trouble," Henry said. "I just came to confess to a murder."

"And who did you kill?" Ray asked.

"Mr. Acorn, one of the owners of Mountain Tours," Henry said.

"He's clean, Chief," Sergeant Toms said after he searched the bank teller.

"Take him back to my office," Ray ordered.

In the chief's office, Ray Wilson put a recorder on his desk and checked to make sure it was loaded with fresh tape. After he started the machine, he sat back in his chair and motioned for Diff and Toms to stay in the room as witnesses. Henry Watson was placed in the chair at the front of the desk.

"Let's start from the top," Ray said. "Why did you kill Mead?"

Henry cleared his throat. "As you know, I am a teller at the bank. The other day Mead came to my window and cashed a large check. I told him to be careful with all that money. He then told me that he was going to work on his plane before going home, but that he had a safe place to hide the bills."

"You killed him for money?" Ray said.

"Yes, sir. I did it out of pure greed. I needed the money because I gamble and have lost so much that I had to steal from the bank. I needed to replace that money I stole, so that's why I killed him."

"How did you do it?" Ray asked.

"I shot him in the head," Henry said. "Don't you want to lock me up now?" He glanced nervously at the telephone on Ray's desk. "I deserve to be locked in a cell without visitors."

"I'll decide who needs to be jailed," Ray said. "Tell me how it happened, Henry. You shot and killed Mead and then flew his plane until it crashed? Is that right?"

"Of course. Lock me up now. I demand to be locked up and thrown in solitary confinement."

"We usually have a trial before we do that," Ray said.

"There's no need for that since I just told you that I did it."

"I would like some more details, Henry. There are a few unexplained items, a minor detail or two that need to be cleared up."

"Like what?" the suspect said. "Ask me anything and I'll answer."

"Okay, let's get this all down. Now . . . let's start with your name, age, address, and place of business."

"Come on, Chief," Henry said. "You've known me for twenty years. I wait on you at the bank. We belong to the same church. You shop in my wife's store and I wait on you there too."

Ray sighed before he said, "Let's just say it is required, Henry. Now, let's start over again with your name . . ."

While Henry Watson answered the routine questions, Diff thought about what he knew of this small man sitting at Ray's desk. The teller was a mild man who had worked at the bank since before Diff came to town. He had never been known to raise his voice, kick a dog, or argue with his wife. He had always seemed to be a model citizen.

Everyone agreed that Henry had to be quiet if he was going to stay married to Doris Watson. Doris was everything that Henry was not. She was a large woman with a loud, brassy voice. She had opinions on everything and let everyone know what they were in no uncertain terms. She ran the 7-Eleven store in Morgan, where she worked during the day. After Henry was through at the bank, he worked in the store until it closed. On weekends, Henry worked in the store from opening to closing. While Henry worked, Doris ate chocolates and watched television.

This mild man's murder of Mead Acorn would point up the evils of too much gambling and how it could change the soul of such a quiet, well-behaved person as Henry Watson.

"Now that we have the prelims over with," Ray said, "let's get on with the murder. You needed the money to make good your gambling losses?"

"That's it, Chief," Henry said. "I lost a bundle."

"At the Indians' casino?" Ray said.

"You got it—a white man scalped by the Indians," Henry said with a phony laugh.

Diff wondered about any scalping since the only time he and Holly had been to the Connecticut casino, the people running the games weren't Native Americans.

"You cashed a large check for Mead and then went down to the dock where you knew he would be," Ray went on.

"Blew his brains out," Henry said with satisfaction. "And then grabbed the dough."

"Where's the money now?" Ray said.

"Went back to the casino and blew that too," Henry said. "Boy, do I deserve jail."

"What did you do with the gun? In other words, where is the murder weapon?" Ray asked.

"Threw it in the middle of Loon Lake," Henry said. "You'll never find it."

Ray looked over at Sergeant Toms with a slight nod that made him leave the room in a hurry. Diff knew a signal had passed and that Ned was now going to check up on one of the details. It wouldn't concern the murder weapon because looking for a gun in the middle of Loon Lake would be an impossible task. There were several other details that needed to be checked out, and Diff wondered which one Ned was tracking first.

"As a matter of curiosity, Henry," Ray said. "Where did you learn to fly?"

"In the army."

"You once told me that you were in army finance."

"That was a coverup for the secret missions I flew for Special Forces. You ought to see my medals," Henry said. "I got some for shooting guns also because I can hit a target at most any distance."

Diff stared at the small man in front of the desk who was confessing to a horrible crime. He had certainly fooled everyone in town. Who would have thought that this mild bank teller, caught in a henpecked marriage, was really a highly trained warrior and pilot?

Ray tented his fingers and looked out the window toward distant trees. For the moment he seemed to be paying little attention to the suspect. "This is all very interesting, Henry, but let's make sure I get it all down right. You shot Mead in the head before you flew the plane into the lake and swam ashore. Is that how it happened?"

"Well, sort of, Chief. I shot him and then did something with the plane for a couple of days before I put it back on Loon Lake for the police to find."

Ray turned his complete attention back to the bank teller. "Well, Henry, why don't you tell me exactly what you did with that plane for a couple of days?"

"Telling you that would get other people in trouble. I admit the killing so you don't need to know any more than that. Throw me in jail and hide the key."

When the phone rang, Henry Watson jumped up and started for the door. "Sit!" Ray commanded before he spoke into the phone in a low voice. He listened for a moment and then hung up to turn his attention back to Henry. "Bank records show that Mead Acorn cashed a check for twenty dollars with you."

Henry turned ash white. "I didn't tell you the amount of the check, did I?"

"You're telling me that you killed Mead for twenty dollars?"

"I was a desperate man. I shot him in the head, so throw me in jail."

The phone rang again. "Yes, Mrs. Watson," Ray said. "Henry is here in my office at this very moment. . . . You say you need him back at the store?"

Henry frantically leaned over the desk. "Tell her I'm in jail for murder. Tell her I won't be able to work in the store—ever again. Tell her that I don't want to ever see that store or her again. . . . No, don't say that. Tell her I can't have visitors because you put killers in solitary confinement."

"He'll be there soon," Ray said as he hung up and shook his head. "You are sentenced to the 7-Eleven store for wasting my time during a murder investigation. Now get out of here."

Diff wrote a note on his pad and handed it to the bank teller as he slinked toward the door: 'You were a Green Beret?'

Henry shook his head. "I paid the soldiers which is like being a bank teller in uniform. I met Doris in the army because she was my first sergeant."

'War is hell,' Diff wrote in his final note to the bank teller.

Ray stood at the window watching Henry hurry down the street. "Is going to jail for life better than living with Doris Watson?"

Diff could write a long note about that, but he knew that he didn't need to.

"We may have one hell of a murder case on our hands, Diff, but I'm also worried about Henry and Doris Watson. Any man who is willing to confess to murder in order to get away from his wife has a real problem."

CHAPTER
5

The Wilsons' living room almost looked as if they were having a small party. Holly had made a big plate of thick roast beef sandwiches surrounded by olives, pickles, and potato chips. There was a slight mountain-air chill so Diff had built a roaring fire in the fireplace. They drank coffee or soft drinks while sitting in a comfortable easy chairs.

It wasn't a party but a brainstorming session with Ray, Sergeant Ned Toms, Sheriff Red Downs, along with Diff and Holly. Sally sat at the table in the corner with a steno pad to take notes of the meeting. Diff had carried the large blackboard from the police station in the back of his pickup truck and placed it along the room's rear wall.

Ray cupped his mug of coffee with both hands. "Okay, the medical examiner says we can't fix the time or place of death, but since Mead lived and worked in Morgan, it's our case. To begin, I think we can start by knocking Henry Watson off our list of suspects. What about that, Ned?"

"Sure thing, Chief," Ned said. The sergeant was a thoughtful man who smoked a pipe and spoke little. When he did make a remark, his words carried weight. "I've checked Henry's army records. He was a soldier clerk with no special forces or flight training. I passed his picture around the gambling casino in Connecticut, and none of the employees can remember seeing him. The bank examiners looked at his records, and he balances to the penny. No teller ever comes that close except Henry. He has an alibi, even if he doesn't want to use it. He was working at the 7-Eleven when the murder took place."

"But we're not sure when it took place," Holly said.

"Doesn't matter when, as far as Henry is concerned," Ned said. "There are a dozen witnesses that say that Henry was either at the bank or working at the store."

"Okay, let's run down the other suspects and find out how this murder could have come down. Diff, do the honors."

Diff went to the blackboard and listed the names of their suspects along with motives:

Mary Acorn, wife of the dead man, possibly killed her husband with the help of her lover, the airport manager. Motive: love and insurance money.

Her friend, Gary Towns, might have done it on his own to get rid of Mead and get at Mead's insurance money.

Ralph Macon, co-owner of Mountain Tours, would benefit from Mead's death since he would become complete owner of the company. He has an alibi but might have arranged with someone for the killing.

Harry Black, owner of Scenic Tours, would be ruined by the success of Mountain Tours. He would be the suspect most interested in revenge.

Henry Watson, bank teller and henpecked husband. No real motive and unlikely killer but has

confessed several times and telephones hourly to
confess again.

Diff finished the list and stepped away from the
blackboard. The room was silent for a while with
everyone's attention turned on the board. "I said to cut
Henry from the list," Ray said. "Erase his name."

Diff removed the name from the board, leaving four
suspects.

"You know," Ray said, "the problem with everyone's
alibi is that we have confusion about when the murder
might have taken place."

"What did the doc say about time of death?" Sheriff
Downs asked as Ned Toms blew a cloud of pipe smoke
rings toward the ceiling.

Diff coughed at the smoke.

Ray looked at his notes. "Uncertain. There were ice
crystals in the body that make him think it might have
been kept in a very cold place."

"You mean like a refrigerator?" Holly asked.

"Yes," her father answered. "That means he cannot tell
the time of death from body temperature. Mead could
have died at any time within a 48-hour period."

"Wow," Holly said. "That really complicates things."

Yeah, wow, Sally thought as she looked over at Diff as
he stretched. *What a hunk!*

Holly glared at Sally with a few bad thoughts about her
former classmate. She couldn't kill Sally in front of her
father and the sheriff—but if looks could kill . . . Diff
didn't realize what was going on between the two women
and kept his attention turned to the list of suspects.

Holly shook her head to break the train of thought
about the other woman and looked at the notes Diff had
given her. "Diff has a couple of questions he wants to ask."

"Shoot," Ray answered.

"Question," she read. "Diff and I saw the plane crash, but a search couldn't find it. Where was it? The plane appeared two days later. Where had it been? How did it rise out of the water? How did a dead man fly the plane?"

"Oh, boy," Ray said. "And I'm supposed to answer those questions with the small force I have?"

"You can give it to the sheriff's department," Ned said.

"Sure can," Red Downs said. "I can call in the state guys to help."

Ray shook his head. "Maybe we'll have to do that later, but as a matter of pride I'd like us to solve our own crimes if we can."

"Like how do we do that, Chief?" Toms said. "We just don't have the manpower."

"We can help," Holly said. "I'm on holiday from teaching the deaf. If you could give Diff a couple of days off, we could work on the case together like we did last time."

It was Sally's turn to glare at Holly with the thought, *Boy, that redhead sure knows her way around. That 'we can do it together' bit was great. I wish I had thought of it. What a spider trap that kid is.*

Ray thought for a few minutes before he spoke. "Okay, you two can have a couple of days to work on the case," he finally said.

Sally stopped admiring Holly and decided to get back in the game. "They can't do that!" she snapped. "They aren't cops."

Ray raised an eyebrow at the clerk. "I am appointing them special officers for this month. I can't make Diff a member of the force because of his handicap, but I can make him a special officer for a short period of time."

Sally thought she would like to see Holly a special officer in a place like upper Alaska.

"First thing in the morning," Ray said, "Holly and Diff start to talk to our suspects. I'll want full reports in writing."

*   *   *

On the following morning Diff and Holly climbed into her sky-blue Saturn and drove to Morgan Airport. As soon as they parked by the office, they heard a deep bark coming from the hangar followed by the sight of a huge dog bounding across the runway toward them. Bushy leaped in the air and knocked Diff over. The dog's large tongue rasped back and forth across Diff's cheeks.

"This time I came prepared," Holly said as she dug in her pocketbook to bring out the biggest dog biscuit Diff had ever seen. "A treat for the largest dog in the world," she said as she flipped the bone in the air.

Bushy leaped up to catch the bone in his teeth. He growled in pleasure as he pinned the biscuit between his front paws and began to go to work on it.

Diff and Holly laughed as they went into the building. Holly wondered how it was that this man by her side could laugh but not speak.

"We're going to be rich!" they heard Mary Acorn yell in glee from the airport office. "Filthy, dirty, stinking rich with a million dollars in insurance money!"

"The sad widow," Holly said. "She can hardly stand her grief."

"Kiss me, darling," they heard her say to Gary as Diff pounded on the door.

"Whoever is there, go away," Gary yelled out in an annoyed voice.

"It's Diff James and Holly Wilson on police business," Holly yelled back.

Gary angrily tore the door open. "Last I heard, you taught at the school for the deaf and Diff mopped floors for a living."

"My father appointed us special officers," Holly said. "Would you like to see our badges?"

"All right, what do you want?"

"To dig into our private business," Mary said from the canvas chair where she pouted.

Diff gave a list of questions to Holly to read aloud. It would be her job to follow the answers with any other necessary questions, if their suspects allowed them to get that far. She read the first one: "We need to know where you each were on the night before the floatplane was discovered on Loon Lake."

"We don't have to answer that," Gary said.

"I can have Dad send a car with armed officers for you," Holly said. "We can talk in a cell as well as here."

"I don't care for your tone of voice," Mary said.

"Please answer the question," Holly said.

"We are not . . ." Mary started to say until Gary broke in.

"If you must know," Gary said, "we were together."

"Where were each of you the day Diff and I saw the plane go down?" Holly pressed.

"They called me at the house and told me you thought you saw the plane go down," Mary said. "I drove over here, which you know because you snooped on Gary and me in this very room that day."

"Before Mary got here, where were you, Gary?" Holly asked.

"In this office all that day. No, I did not fly the floatplane or kill Mead."

"So why don't you two just get out of here?" Mary said. "We're getting sick of being spied on by busybody creeps."

"Boy, aren't they a sweet couple?" Holly said when they were outside walking toward the Mountain Tours building. "It seems that Mary was home the day we saw the crash, but Gary has no real alibi."

Diff smiled and wrote a note to her: 'Outside of that and the fact that they have a double motive—insurance money and a love affair—what else do we have on them?'

"What we have, my friend," Holly said, "is the important fact that the murderer had to know how to fly an airplane. Our friend with the rotten manners is also a pilot."

'A pilot with half an alibi,' Diff wrote. All the other suspects were also trained pilots too. They approached the Mountain Tours building and looked in the window to see Ralph Macon. The dead man's partner was in a small office speaking to the Laman brothers in a voice too low for them to hear.

Luke Laman held out his hand for Ralph to slap a large wad of money in his palm. Joe Laman snatched the money away from his brother and carefully counted it.

"Those brothers are up to no good again," Holly whispered to Diff. "They're always breaking the law and getting away with it. They don't have regular jobs, but they always seem to have money."

Diff had first met the brothers right after his arrival in town. The Lamans seemed to take particular joy in pushing him toward a fight, making fun of him, or doing a dozen other things to make him unhappy. He'd seen them steal gasoline from cars, and he knew they were hunting and fishing illegally. They were always after an easy dollar. The question today was, why was Ralph Macon paying them a large amount of money?

The Laman brothers waved at Ralph and left the

building by the door near the runway. Diff and Holly watched their pickup speed toward the highway and take the turn with a screech of tires.

The Mountain Tours partner seemed tense and surprised to see them. There were lines of worry on his face, while his hands had a slight shake to them. A smell of whiskey was on his breath. "This is sort of a bad time for me, guys. There will be no free rides today. I have problems now that my partner is dead and the floatplane is all busted up."

"My father wants us to talk with you," Holly said. "That makes this official business."

Ralph rubbed his eyes with the back of his hand. "Okay, okay, but I'm bushed. What is it you want to know?"

Diff wrote rapid notes that Holly read to Ralph as quickly as he handed them to her. "Did you get your contracts?" she asked.

"Sure did. Only good thing to come out of this mess. Starting next month, Mountain Tours will more than triple in size."

"We know you were piloting the plane with us in it when we saw the floatplane go down, but where were you the night before it was found?"

"In New York City. I have about twenty people who saw me down there both in the hotel and at the airlines office. Want their names?"

"Send them over to my father if you will," Holly said. As they left the Mountain Tours building Holly turned to Diff. "Well, I think we can say that Ralph has two good alibis. One is us—he was piloting us the time we saw the plane go down. His other alibi is his trip to New York."

Diff wrote a one page note. 'Lamans,' it read.

"Sure. The brothers could have been hired by Ralph,

but remember, you're the one who said the murderer had to be a pilot. How about that? Those brothers never finished high school, much less took pilot training."

Harry Black stood in the doorway of the Scenic Tours building and watched them approach. "Got a telephone call from Gary, who said you two were snooping around asking questions about the killing."

"That we are," Holly asked.

"Well, I have no alibi for the whole week. I worked and slept in here, working on my books. I'm fighting to keep Mountain Tours from driving me out of business."

"Are you angry about that?" Holly asked.

"Damn tooting I'm mad about it," Harry said.

"Enough to kill a man for revenge?" Holly pressed.

"I don't quite think so, young lady. If you're suggesting I wrote that word in blood on the plane window, you are nuts. Please excuse me—I have to go back to work."

Bushy had finished his dog bone and galloped toward Diff, nearly knocking Harry Black down. "Damn mutt!" Harry said as he tried to kick the dog.

Holly put her hand on Diff's shoulder as he started forward to protect the large dog. "No, don't," she said. "Bushy's all right. Look at him run off."

"Dog ought to be put out of his misery," Harry said as he slammed the door to his office.

Diff looked at the closed door and wondered about the man who kicked dogs.

CHAPTER
6

Diff tacked a large map of Mohawk County on his wall. Loon Lake was nearly in its center with the town of Morgan in the lower, right-hand corner. Few roads crossed over the mountains and through the forests, and some lakes were not on any roads.

He sat in front of the map and tried to think. He had taken the plane ride with Holly on Saturday. They had watched the floatplane go down in the center of the lake. A search of the area had not located the wreck. Another mystery was how that plane had been found floating quietly on the surface of the water two days later. Not only had the plane been filled with water, but damage made it look like it had crashed.

Diff and Holly both saw the plane go down. One person could have been mistaken, but not two. They saw a crash that search divers could not find. It didn't make any sense at all. . . . Unless the men doing the underwater search had lied. If they had found the sunken airplane

52

but had not reported it, that would solve part of the mystery. That still did not explain the puzzle of how the plane had been found on the surface two days later.

All the divers were police officers of one sort or another led by Sergeant Toms, who was as honest as anyone in the state. Why would they lie, and how would the killer have reached them? Diff did not think the divers had been paid off. He believed they hadn't found the plane because it wasn't there.

He attacked the problem from another angle. If the plane had not crashed and they had been tricked in some manner . . . where had the airplane been for a couple of days? Several people saw the floatplane take off early Saturday morning and fly over Bald Mountain. It had been lost from sight until hours later when Diff and Holly saw it crash.

If the floatplane took off at dawn and did not crash until later, where had it been for seven hours? It could not stay in the air all that time since a full tank of gas only gave it four hours of flying time.

The airplane with the body of Mead Acorn had to land on water and take off again to fly back to Loon Lake. Finding where it had been for those missing hours might be a good place to start.

He looked at the map with a magnifying glass. The plane was seen to fly over Bald Mountain, so he looked at the wilderness area on the far side of that map feature. There weren't any roads in that area, only woods and two lakes.

He knew the plane was often used to ferry fisherman into those distant lakes. It was possible that Mead was making such a flight the day he was killed. However, Mountain Tour records did not show any lake trips for that day. As far as anyone knew, Mead was alone in the plane when it took off.

Diff drew a route on the map. If they drove to Bald
Mountain and picked up the Jones River near the
foothills, they could canoe down the rapids to Lake
Walpie. They would have to carry the canoe over to Lake
Jasper east of that. It would be a tough hike, but it could
be done. It would be at least a two-day trip, so they
would need food, a tent, and sleeping bags.

Diff dropped his pencil when he realized he was
thinking in terms of *we* and *us*. He knew who that meant,
because Holly Wilson was the only other person in the
world who fit.

*   *   *

"You want me to go camping with you?" Holly asked
after she read his note. "Just the two of us?"

He nodded.

"Diff, I know when you came to Morgan you had to learn
a great many things about life, but I thought you knew that
a man and woman, a boy and a girl . . . well, people of the
opposite sex just don't go off camping alone together unless
they are . . . well, lovers. You know what I mean?"

Diff wrote as fast as he could and gave her the result.
'I'm sorry. I didn't mean it that way,' she read. 'I don't
want you to think that I was pulling something. We need
to look into where the floatplane might have landed.
We've been doing this case together so I thought we
could explore this together.'

"Dad had to go away to a state police meeting for
three days," Holly said. "I'll go if you give me your word
nothing will happen."

'I give my word,' Diff wrote neatly on his pad and
gave her the sheet.

Holly looked down at his message and tried to hide
her disappointment. She knew he would keep to his

word, for that was very important to him. She had to admit she sometimes wished he wasn't quite so honorable. "Then let's get our stuff together and go in your pickup," she said with a forced laugh.

*   *   *

They parked at the Jones River boat-launching area in the foothills of Bald Mountain. Diff unloaded the canoe from the pickup and locked the truck as Holly put their pack in the center of the boat. When everything was ready, Diff sat in the rear with Holly at the bow.

They used their paddles to gently push the canoe away from shore and then let the fast current from Bald Mountain carry them downstream. From time to time Diff had to paddle on one side or the other to keep the canoe on a straight heading, but the river current did most of the work.

If their mission hadn't been so serious, it would have been a great canoe trip. The water ran cold and fresh as it rushed off the mountain toward the forest lake. Sun spotted the water when it broke through the trees, revealing dashing trout. The river was a shallow four feet with a clearly visible bottom of sand and polished pebbles. Hanging trees and brush along the banks gave their passage a tunnel-like appearance.

They heard the loud rush of water in the distance. "White water ahead," Holly said.

Diff nodded because he knew the river well and had shot these rapids before. If he could speak, he'd yell at her to hold on tight. The warning probably wasn't needed since Holly was an experienced canoeist and knew what to do. He hoped they didn't capsize and get their food and bedding wet and soggy.

Holly gave an excited yell. "Here we go!"

The canoe shot between two large boulders where water

bubbled white foam as it struck the rocks. Diff could see the channel far ahead as he paddled hard to go between the rocks to hit open water. If they turned to the side, water would pour into the canoe and quickly swamp them. That was dangerous, for even if the river wasn't deep, the rapid current could sweep you off your feet and slam you against rocks. Men and women had died along here when they were swept down the channel by the rushing water.

Their canoe finally shot through an opening in the rapids into flat water.

"We made it!" Holly screamed in excitement. "Oh, wow!"

After the rapids, the river calmed as it flowed into Lake Walpie. When they entered the lake, the quiet day closed around them. A distant bird gave a lonely cry to signal they were deep in the forest where the steps of men were rare and roads or houses were distant.

They slowly paddled around the edge of Lake Walpie. On the north bank was a single log cabin with a rotting dock. Diff knew this was the Walpie Fish Camp. Mountain Tours flew fishermen here while occasional others made the white-water canoe trip into the lake.

Diff and Holly pulled the canoe ashore at the camp and walked to the sagging front porch. The cabin door was held shut by a wooden crossbar. Inside the cabin they found that leaves had blown through a broken window and dust had covered the table and part of the floor. The lack of footprints made it obvious that no one had been in the cabin since last summer.

They returned to the canoe and finished their circle around the lake. A steep bluff rose from the water's edge along the west shore. It would be hard, if not impossible, for anyone to climb the bluff from that approach. There were only a few other places to dock a seaplane. When Diff checked each one, he found no track signs that showed any human had been here since last summer. 'Let's go,' he wrote on a note to Holly.

"Lake Jasper next stop," she said as they paddled to the head of the narrow trail that connected the two lakes. Holly settled the heavy pack on her back, while Diff pulled the canoe over his shoulders. He gripped the sides with both hands for balance as they started down the path toward the other lake.

It was a two-mile portage to Lake Jasper. During the last mile Diff began to breathe heavily although he was in excellent condition. The canoe was not that heavy, but its size made it awkward to carry since it threw off his stride.

"Want me to carry that while you take the pack for awhile?" Holly asked.

Diff shook his head.

"Okay, we're almost there."

Lake Jasper was a beautiful spot, filled with fat fish and surrounded by animals that roamed free and safe from men with guns. Most fishermen would not make the difficult hike they had just made, so the only other way to get into the area was by plane. There was no fish-camp cabin here, but they knew of a level area across the lake where a tent could be pitched and a canoe pulled ashore. There was a wall of boulders at the rear of the site that gave it some protection from wind and storms. Over the years campers had built a loose stone fireplace and cut large logs that provided furniture of a sort.

They put their canoe in the water with the pack in the center and began to paddle across the quiet lake.

They were midway across when they heard the drone of a powerful airplane engine. Holly was in the bow of the canoe facing back toward Diff. He looked toward a hill at their front which seemed to be the direction of the plane.

"That doesn't sound like anything we have at Morgan Airport," Holly said.

She was right. Although it was obviously a single-engine craft, it had the powerful throb sound of a fighter plane.

Diff stopped paddling as the plane came over the hill and flew toward them at treetop level. It was not like any plane he had ever seen land in Morgan, but it was similar to an exhibit he had seen at the Connecticut Aircraft Museum. It looked like a World War II P-40 fighter plane.

Four spots on the wings seemed to be winking at him.

"Boy, the fish are really jumping out here," Holly said. "You ought to see them splash."

Then the sound reached them. Over the roar of the powerful engine they heard the slamming bangs of machine-gun fire.

The plane roared overhead only a few feet above them. When it reached the end of the lake, it banked steeply to make another pass.

Holly looked puzzled as she stared up at the turning plane. "What's going on?" she asked. "Why is he buzzing us like that?"

Diff knew what was happening. The winks of light coming from the plane were machine-gun fire from the aircraft's wing guns. The pilot of that ancient plane was trying to kill them. What Holly thought were splashing fish were the impacts of .50-caliber machine-gun shells.

The plane's tight turn would soon have it in position to roar back down the lake for a second go at them. He had overshot on the first pass, but the pilot would correct his fire on the second try until machine-gun bullets ripped through their bodies.

CHAPTER 7

Diff stood in the canoe and threw his paddle in the direction of the onrushing fighter plane. The wing guns began to wink their deadly eyes again as bullets chewed the shore and walked across the water.

"What are you doing?" Holly screamed. "You can't stand in a canoe!"

In seconds the march of machine-gun fire would rip through their bodies. They were in the middle of the lake without cover, which meant they didn't have a chance.

"Get down, Diff!" Holly yelled as she stood to face the rushing plane. When she realized what was happening she turned toward Diff in terror. "What is he—?"

Diff could not give the quick warning she needed if she were to live. There was no time to write a long note to explain that in seconds they were going to die.

He did the only thing he could and hit Holly hard on the point of her chin. Her eyes rolled back in her head as she tumbled over the side of the boat and sank.

Bullets pocked the lake as they reached their deadly claws forward at a speed of two hundred and fifty miles an hour. He pretended to be hit and threw up his hands and fell over the side of the boat as if mortally wounded. The canoe turned over as Diff sank under the deep waters of the lake.

Holly was still unconscious twenty feet below the surface when he reached her. The clear lake revealed the thunk of the long shells as they spattered in the water or holed the overturned canoe. He grabbed Holly by the hair and kicked toward the surface.

He saw the dim glow of the sun as he swam toward the surface as strongly as he could. He knew they could not come out in open water as that would alert the pilot, who would be watching to make sure his shots had succeeded. If they were seen on the surface of the lake, they would never reach shore before the plane made another pass over them with guns firing.

There was only one possible chance and he knew that when he had deliberately capsized. The canoe floated above them and he surfaced inside the overturned craft.

He held Holly by the waist as his bicycling legs kept them afloat under the canoe. She began to sputter and cough as she turned in his arms.

"You hit me," she said through another cough. When her throat cleared, she ducked underwater to swim out from under the canoe.

Diff scissored his feet around her waist to stop her escape. That brought her head inches from his face.

"What are you doing? You promised there'd be no funny stuff. . . ."

He shook his head and cupped his ear.

Holly began to scissor her legs to help keep them both afloat. They heard machine-gun fire chewing up the dirt at the campsite as bullets whined off the windbreak rocks.

"Someone was shooting at us," she said in amazement. "They were trying to kill us, so you hit me to knock me underwater."

He nodded.

"Thanks," Holly said as she threw both arms around him and kissed him on the mouth.

They sank until they were forced to break apart to swim back under the canoe. They listened as the plane fought for altitude. Then the sound lowered as the whine of the airplane engine faded in the distance.

They righted the canoe and pushed it toward the campsite on the far shore. When they were able to touch bottom, they staggered up the small beach and fell, exhausted, facedown on the ground.

When her breathing returned to normal, Holly turned to support her head on a hand as she smiled at Diff. "You're wondering how anyone knew we were out here," Holly said. "It's all my fault because I made a dumb mistake. I never dreamed anyone wanted to kill us, so I left a note for Daddy on the screen door. I told him where we were going and when we would be back. Anyone who drove by the house could see the note and read it and know exactly where we were. It was dumb of me, Diff, and I'm sorry. But I never dreamed . . ."

Diff couldn't say it, but he feared they were going to pay for her little mistake. Their food, bedding, and tent had sunk to the bottom of the lake when he turned the canoe over. It was going to be a long and hungry night. Even at this time of year it was cold at night in the mountains. They were going to be a bit uncomfortable.

It was also obvious that the campsite would give them little comfort. The ground was torn up by machine-gun bullets. Brush and small trees had been blasted apart until leaves and branches covered the ripped earth. It looked as if not only had the fighter plane tried to kill them, but the pilot had deliberately shot up the campsite in order to destroy evidence.

Holly shivered as she sat hugging her knees. "Okay, Mr. Woodsman, you're supposed to be the survival expert. Let's see what you can do for us with this little gizmo." She handed him her Swiss Army knife.

With that handy knife in his possession, Diff was able to do a great many things. Gathering wood was quite easy since the machine gun had created a ready supply within reach. Holly laid a fire while Diff used the knife's small magnifying glass turned to the sun to spark a tiny pile of wood shavings. He shortly had a nice campfire for Holly.

While Holly warmed by the fire, Diff used the knife to cut a five-foot spear, which he sharpened to a point on one end. He stopped work every few minutes to listen for the sound of an approaching airplane. They were probably safe from land intruders this far out in the woods, but it would be smart to listen for the sound of a plane engine. If they heard one coming, they would have time to run deep into the surrounding woods and hide.

He waded into the lake until water was just above his knees. He patiently raised the spear over his head while he looked into the shallow water. The rarely visited lake was filled with fat fish, and within fifteen minutes Diff was able to spear a plump bass. In a few more minutes he had it cleaned, sliced, and roasting over the fire.

*   *   *

After they had eaten and he had gathered more firewood, they sat next to each other, looking into the dancing flames.

"It would be almost romantic if things were a little different," Holly said.

He knew she said that because it was expected. If she were with a real boyfriend, they would be in each other's arms now and would fall asleep warm and close.

He felt her leg against his knee and he moved slightly away. In a few moments he could feel her leg again. He knew she hadn't meant to do it, but all he could think about was her nearness. Diff jumped to his feet and started looking for more wood.

"We have plenty of that stuff," Holly said. "Come back to the fire."

He sat back down by the fire, on the side opposite Holly.

What's wrong with me? Holly thought. *Is he nice to me only because my father has done him many favors? I wish I knew.*

They finally curled up on opposite sides of the fire for a night of broken sleep.

*   *   *

Early the next morning when they went to leave camp, they found the canoe sitting underwater. The gunshot holes had taken their toll. It was going to be a long hike back to the truck.

"We're going to have to walk completely around the lake, aren't we?" Holly asked.

Diff nodded and took her hand to begin the difficult hike around the lake. After they reached the far side, they would take the wandering trail back to Lake Walpie. Then they would walk along the riverbank to Bald Mountain and the pickup truck.

At least it would be easy to find their attacker, Diff thought. How many World War II P-40 fighter planes that were in flying condition could there be in the whole country? There couldn't be more than half a dozen. It would be easy work to locate the aircraft, trace its owner, and arrest him for attempted murder. They would probably find a strong link between the pilot of the fighter plane and the person who killed Mead Acorn. The case was practically solved.

*   *   *

A day and a half later Diff and Holly hiked back to Bald Mountain and tiredly climbed into the waiting pickup. The drive back to Morgan took them past the airport. Diff's estimate was right. There were six P-40 fighter planes in flying condition in the country—and five of them were now neatly lined up on the runway at Morgan Airport.

The truck fishtailed as Diff quickly turned into the airport drive and drove up to the office. He braked and turned off the engine to sit looking at the parked planes. All five P-40s were exactly like the machine that had nearly killed them the day before.

"This is not to say that I don't love lake fish three meals a day," Holly said. "But I am dying to sink my fangs into some red meat. I'm starved." She held up a wadded ten-dollar bill. "Look what I found in my pocket that survived all our adventures."

Diff's answer was to climb from the truck and open her door. He gave a deep bow and extended his hand.

"Thank you, sir," Holly said. "Food first, and then I'm going to climb into a hot tub and just soak for about three hours."

Diff pointed to the antique airplanes lined up along the runway.

"Right, a tub bath after we find out about those airplanes and who it was who shot at us."

A few minutes later, while munching a juicy hamburger, Holly struck up a conversation with the cook at the airport snack bar.

"Where did those planes out there on the runway come from?" she asked. "And where are the pilots?"

"They flew in yesterday on their way to the air show at Rhinebeck," Lacey, the short-order cook, said. "You still look hungry, Diff. Want me to throw another burger on the grill?"

When Diff nodded, Lacey flipped a meat patty on the hot grill. "Yep, those babies roared in here early yesterday and the pilots all checked into the Idle Hours Motel. They were swimming and having a great party until someone snuck out here and stole one of the planes. Boy, was that owner mad. The cops still haven't found the thing. I mean, how hard is it to hide something as big as a fifty-year-old airplane?"

"Do they have any idea who might have stolen the plane?" Holly asked.

"Not a clue," Lacey said as he flipped the burger on a bun and handed the plate to Diff.

Later when Diff went to police headquarters to write a report on the attempted murder, Sally Way waved him down at the reception desk. She picked up her steno pad. "Got a call for you and the chief from that guy at Mountain Tours, Ralph what's-his-name," she said. "He says you won't need to bother checking with the airline people he met with in New York. He says he's figured out what happened to the plane you and Holly saw go down. He said you, the chief, and the sheriff are to come to the Mountain Tours office tomorrow at three, and he'll give you a demonstration of what happened."

Diff took the page from her pad.

"Now, if you want to interview people, Diff," Sally said,

"why don't you start with me? I'd really like to have a personal interview with you—maybe right now down in the boiler room."

"How about right now in a holding cell?" Holly said loudly as she entered the building.

"You don't have a bit of humor in you," Sally said with a pout as she answered a phone call.

When Diff and Holly entered the office, it was obvious from Chief Ray Wilson's body language that he was angry. They were surprised to find that part of the anger was directed at them. "I go away on business for a couple of days, and you two dance off to the woods to play games. Then some crazy guys land a bunch of World War II airplanes in Morgan and an even crazier guy steals one of them. If I didn't know they weren't bright enough, I'd blame the theft on the Laman brothers. I should have stayed home."

"Are you mad at us for investigating on our own, which, I might point out, you asked us to do?" Holly asked.

"Let's just say that I'm an old-fashioned guy who's just beginning to realize what's been going on under my own roof."

"What are you talking about, Daddy?"

"I've been informed about the town gossip concerning you two. Which, I might point out, you don't help by running off to the woods to play campers. I don't care how things are these days with other men and women. What they do privately is their business. Like I said, I'm old-fashioned when it comes to my own family."

"And I happen to be over twenty-one," Holly snapped back.

"You might be, but you also live in my house. As long as you are under my roof, I would prefer that you not have the morals of an alley cat."

"Daddy, are you suggesting—?"

"I'm not suggesting anything. I've just found out what's been going on in my own home by a man I thought was my friend. I got an anonymous letter when I got back to town which made certain statements about you two. I talked to your friend Sally. At first she didn't want to pass on any gossip, but I insisted. She took the time to fill me in about you two. I want you to move, Diff. You are not welcome on my property any longer."

"Wait just a minute! What Sally told you are lies!"

Holly's anger was interrupted by a phone call. Her father snatched the receiver angrily. "What? . . . Right!" He slammed the phone down. "That was Sergeant Toms. They found the stolen P-40 parked in Jim Bean's cornfield."

Diff ran from the room and down the hall to the rear door, which opened out to the parking lot. He had to reach that plane before its owner arrived. He would have to leave it up to Holly to square things with Ray.

He drove toward the east side of town as fast as the law would allow. He knew that the Bean farm consisted of two hundred acres of good bottomland located along the river. The farmer was a quiet man who spoke little and kept to himself except for one day a year when he opened his pumpkin patch for children to gather free pumpkins.

After a search of the farm, Diff found Jim Bean standing on the edge of the south forty, which was planted in corn. The lanky farmer scratched his head as he looked at the World War II fighter plane sitting in the middle of his field. The plane's landing had cut a wide path through the corn down the center of the field.

Diff handed the farmer a note. 'Did you see the pilot?' it read.

"Nope," Bean answered.

'When did it land?' was Diff's next question.

"Yesterday," was the crisp answer. "Heard it, but didn't find it until today."

Diff walked over to the plane and felt along the wing-gun ports. The barrels were now cold, but the smell of gunpowder was still there. These guns had been fired recently. This was the same plane that had tried to kill them.

The hand that fell on his shoulder made him turn with his fists balled. He dropped his combat posture when he saw that it was Ray Wilson. The police chief looked at him with dark eyes as his right hand brushed along the leather of his waist holster.

Diff stepped back and then stopped stock-still. If his best friend wanted to do him harm, he would not run.

Ray Wilson's stern face softened into a smile. "Holly told me about your camping trip and how you saved her life when you were attacked. She also told me about a recent talk she had with Sally about you two. It doesn't take a police genius to figure out where that mysterious letter came from. I respect your word, Diff, so I'm asking if there's been anything between you and Holly?"

Diff wrote 'No' on the note that he gave to Ray.

"I believe you," Ray said, "so let's get back to work." He walked slowly around the fighter plane. "This is an old one," Ray said when he completed his tour. "It looks to me like some sort of World War II fighter plane like the other ones parked at the airport. It's a miracle you two weren't killed. What that means is that someone knew you were out there and was afraid you might find something."

Diff wrote a long note and handed it to Ray.

Ray read, 'The floatplane might have been moored

there during the two days it was missing. The plane attack was not only meant to kill us. It also was to destroy any tracks or clues at the campsite.'

They walked slowly back to their vehicles. Ray stopped by the door of his police cruiser and watched Diff drive away in his pickup. He believed Diff's one-word note that said, ' No.' Now that his anger had cooled, he realized that, in a way, he was slightly disappointed. Not that he wanted things going on under his roof, but he would not be sad if his daughter and Diff became romantically involved.

D iff drove around the Bean
farm, looking for the clue he knew was hidden there
somewhere. The pilot who tried to kill them on the lake
flew the fighter plane to this farm, abandoned it in the
cornfield, and then fled back to town. That meant
transportation had to be available within an easy walk of
the landing spot. In addition to being handy, the pilot
would hide the car or truck to make sure that it wasn't
easily noticed.

If there was a clue here, he would find it. He drove
along the highway that ran along one side of the farm.
Corn and other crops lined the road, but it was too early
in the season for crops to be high enough to hide a car or
truck. He drove down the dirt road that ran along the
west side of the farm. It passed over the river that
marked the northern boundary of the property.

He drove slowly across the narrow wooden bridge to
the far side. There was a side road that ran down the

bank to the water's edge. He stopped his truck and walked down the path.

The road down to the river was really only two narrow ruts, but they were wide enough to drive a car down. He followed the path down to the river, where it turned under the bridge.

There were tire tracks in the river mud and clay under the bridge. Diff knelt and felt the markings. A heavy rain three days ago would have washed these tracks away if they were here then. That meant that someone had parked a vehicle, probably a small four-by-four, under this bridge during the last three days.

The clay under the bridge was very unusual and not very common in the Mohawk County area. He knelt to feel the clay with his fingers.

This was the clue he was looking for. It would be very interesting to find if either of their suspects had clay similar to this caught in the treads of his tires.

*   *   *

Holly walked into the Morgan Bar and Grill and sat on a stool midway down the bar. Four Eyes Marlee, the bartender, kept polishing the same beer glass over and over again while he stared at Holly. Finally he put the glass down and walked over to stand in front of her.

"Diff isn't here, Miss Wilson. Only customers we got today are those guys down at the end." He bent his head toward the end of the bar where the Laman brothers were talking quietly to each other. "You don't want to be around here when those bad apples notice you."

"I can take care of myself, Mr. Marlee."

"Maybe yes, maybe no, but I don't want any trouble with your dad. You know what I mean?"

Luke Laman waved his hand at Four Eyes to signal for

another beer. He stopped with his hand still in the air as he stared at Holly.

"Well, lookee who's here," Luke said as he poked his brother in the ribs. "It's Miss Goody Three Shoes, the Retard's girlfriend."

"That's Goody Two Shoes, Luke," Holly yelled down the bar. "Either of you lunkheads care to buy a girl a sandwich?"

Joe Laman catapulted off his stool and strode up the bar toward Holly. "Baby, you can have anything your little heart desires," he said as he put his arm around Holly.

"Watch it, Joe," Marlee said. "I don't want her daddy mad at me and closing me down over trouble with his daughter."

"No trouble, Mr. Marlee," Holly said. "Can you make me a sandwich?"

"Only got ham and cheese," the bartender said.

"Fine with me," Holly said as she slipped out of Joe's arm and went to a corner booth.

When Joe Laman tried to slide into the booth with her, his way was blocked by his brother. "I saw her first," Luke said. "Go check the truck or something."

"You're history, Luke," Joe said. "Now beat it or you'll get hurt."

These are two really lovely guys, Holly thought to herself as Marlee put a sandwich in front of her. Joe Laman whipped a wad of bills from his pocket and peeled off a ten, which he handed to the bartender. "Keep the change, Four Eyes."

"I said, I saw her first," Luke said as he twirled his brother around.

"Hey, come on, guys," Holly said. "Both of you sit down."

The Laman brothers glared at each other for a moment as if undecided as to who should attack first until Luke made a lopsided smile. "She's woman enough for both of us," he said as he slid into the booth across from Holly. "Where's Speak No Evil today?" he asked.

Holly shrugged. "Who knows? I'm not Diff's keeper. Now, you guys are the kind of action men I can appreciate."

"Hey ya!" Luke yelled as he slapped his brother on the shoulder. "We got ourselves a live one."

Holly wasn't really hungry and played with her sandwich as she smiled across the booth at the brothers. "You paid that guy a ten for a ham sandwich worth three bucks at most?"

"Easy come, easy go," Joe Laman said.

"I like guys who really know how to make a buck without working much," Holly said.

Luke thought about this for a moment, which caused him to look at Holly with a trace of suspicion. "Your daddy send you down here to talk to us?"

"Nope."

"I mean, does he have us in mind as suspects on any little you-know-what, little robberies in town?"

"Nope."

"What's your game, Holly?" Luke continued. "You didn't come into this dump to order a ham sandwich."

"Maybe I came for action, Luke Boy," Holly said. "I might be willing to really play and have a good time if you have the money to show me around. Do you get that, or do I draw you a picture?"

"What about me?" Joe asked.

"I want a steak dinner, a bunch of drinks, and then I want to dance all night," Holly said. "But to do all that I need a new outfit with pocketbook, shoes, and maybe a new pair of earrings."

"That could be arranged," Luke said as he pulled a large wad of money from his pocket. "Look at these babies that are hot to trot to buy a steak and a new outfit for a pretty redhead."

"Hey," Holly said with wonder. "Where did you get all that? I mean, since you guys don't have a steady job and all . . . where did you get it?"

"Just say we did a special job for a friend of ours who was very, very grateful," Joe said.

"Like who?" Holly asked through a mouthful of sandwich she chewed in order to appear casual.

"Like a man who runs airplanes to look at the pretty hills," Joe said. "Ow! Hey, watch it, Luke. You kicked me."

"Because you have a big mouth," his brother answered.

"Like what sort of job pays that kind of money?" Holly asked with her eyes on her sandwich. "I mean, did you have to kill somebody or something?"

"You know, pretty lady," Luke said, "you ask a lot of questions."

"Just wondering where you got the dough," Holly said as she edged toward the corner of the booth.

"We didn't kill no one," Joe said. "What we did was—"

Diff burst through the door. While his eyes adjusted to the dim light inside the bar, he handed the bartender a note as Holly slumped down in the booth.

"Hey, Laman brothers," Marlee yelled across the room. "Diff here wants to know if you know where Holly is? He writes that her car is parked outside."

"We don't know nothing," Joe called back.

Diff started toward the booth as Marlee pulled a baseball bat out from under the bar. "I don't want no trouble," Marlee said as he reached for the telephone with the other hand and punched in 9ll.

*   *   *

Holly got her steak an hour later, but she had to put it on Diff's black eye as they parked outside Morgan Airport. "You know," she said, "that was tonight's dinner. If you hadn't come barging in, I might have gotten some information from the Lamans. I think Joe was about to tell me something because he was in a bragging mood. Well, there's no use in crying over spilled beer, is there?"

'Spilled milk,' Diff wrote on his pad and handed to Holly.

"I know," she said, "but with the Lamans it's got to be spilled beer. What next?"

Some of the anger Diff had directed toward the Lamans now spilled over toward Holly. He could not understand why she was in that bar in the first place. He wrote a note so fast that he snapped the pencil before he handed it to her. 'Why?'

Holly read it and answered. "I told you. I was going to get some info from the Laman brothers."

He managed to scribble a note with the stub of his pencil that read, 'You know those guys have a thing going with me. They might have done something to you just to get back at me.'

It was Holly's turn to be angry. "If you don't want my help, let's get out of here. Take me home."

They glared at each other for a moment until Holly put her hand on his arm. "Let's not be mad at each other, okay?"

He nodded and handed her another note. 'I want to check the cars and trucks parked here to see if there's a certain type of red clay stuck in their tire treads.'

Holly took the steak off his eye and jumped from the car to throw the beef high in the air. A bounding animal sped across the yard and leaped up to catch the steak in his large mouth. "I knew it wouldn't go to waste with Bushy around," she said sadly.

There were six cars and trucks parked in the parking lot by the office and snack bar. Diff crawled under each one while Holly kept a lookout.

After he climbed under the last pickup, a dusty Dodge with "Morgan Airport" lettering on its side, Diff stood and held out his hand for Holly to see the lumps of red clay on his fingers.

"It's from under the river bridge at the Bean farm, isn't it?" she said.

A quick examination of the truck discovered an olive-drab ammo box. The army lettering on its side stated that it had once contained A-l .50-caliber belted ammunition.

"Can't you buy those boxes at almost any army-navy store and a lot of hardware stores? I think Daddy has one in the cellar that he uses for tool storage."

Diff raised an eyebrow.

Holly gave a short laugh. "Okay, where there's smoke, there might be evidence of machine-gun ammo. Right?"

They decided to search the airport's hangar first. Bushy was the watchdog for the building, but since Diff and Holly were just about his favorite persons, not a bark was heard.

Diff directed Holly to search the left side of the building while he took the right. She began to carefully go through the tool benches and equipment stored there. "I wish I knew what the stuff we're searching for looks like," she said.

Diff didn't have to tell her because she would know if she found any.

They spent over an hour going through the hangar without results. "This is a no-go, Diff," Holly finally said as she tiredly leaned against an aircraft whose engine had been removed. "If there's any evidence of ammunition in here, I just don't see it."

Diff scratched Bushy's ears as the dog's tail thumped against the floor. Finding evidence of the ammunition in the hangar was probably too much to expect although he felt certain they had searched the hanger thoroughly. He beckoned to Holly.

"We're going, right?"

He nodded and gave a final pat to the dog as they started for the side door. Bushy tilted his head as they began to leave and then curled on his blanket by the door. He laid his huge head on a paw and looked up at them with sad eyes.

Diff went over to give the friendly dog one last pet. As he bent over to scratch a dog ear he saw it. The copper tip of the large bullet was poking out of a fold in the blanket. He carefully pulled back the blanket to reveal a single .50-caliber shell resting partially under the dog's tail.

"How in the world did that get there?" Holly asked. "I bet Bushy found it and was playing with it, which is why it's in his blanket."

*   *   *

"I don't care what you found in my truck or sticking out of a blanket in the dog bed!" The airport manager was so angry his body shook. "In the first place, anyone could have used the airport truck. If you'd kept on looking, you would have seen that the keys are in the ignition. Lots of us use it. My mechanics use it to haul stuff. The snack bar people use it to get supplies. We use it to lead planes over to the gasoline pump. It's a truck that a dozen people can get at."

Holly held up the machine-gun shell. "And this was found in your hangar."

"In a dog bed!" Gary nearly screamed. "Anyone could have put it there."

And without fingerprints, Diff thought to himself.

Chief Wilson stood with his arms folded as he looked across his office at the angry Gary. "It's not enough for an arrest," he finally said in a low voice. "But it's getting pretty close, Gary. Not only did you have motive to kill Mead Acorn, but you are a flyer, and now we find deadly ammunition in your hangar. We get anything else against you and you'll be arrested, so if you want to deal, now is the time to do it."

"Am I free to go?" Gary put his hand on the door handle, eager to escape.

"You are," Ray said.

"Then do me a favor and keep these two snoopers away from my airport. Okay?" He went out, slamming the door.

"The evidence points in his direction," Ray said. "But we have to move carefully or he can bring a lawsuit against us."

"He's the one, Daddy," Holly insisted. "The airport van was parked out at the Bean farm where the fighter plane landed. The plane that tried to kill us was firing .50-caliber machine guns—the same as the live shell we found in the airport hanger."

"Without an eyewitness we have to have more against him," Ray said. "I just don't have enough for an arrest at this point."

Diff thought back to the day he and Holly had seen the floatplane crash. Ralph had radioed the Morgan Airport for help and someone had phoned the emergency squads. Who had taken that call? If Gary was at the radio, he couldn't have been the killer. . . . That was something that had to be looked into.

CHAPTER
9

The leather chairs and sofa in the small waiting room of Mountain Tours had been lined up in front of a fish tank. The tank's former occupants now swam in buckets that sat along the rear wall. The guests began to arrive. Sheriff Downs of Mohawk County came with two deputies. Morgan Police Chief Ray Wilson had his assistant, Sergeant Ned Toms. Diff and Holly had also been asked to watch Ralph Macon's demonstration. They were the next to last to arrive and sat together on the sofa.

Sally Way, carrying her steno pad, was the last to arrive. She looked around the small room for a place to sit. There weren't any vacant chairs so she stood in front of the sofa and cleared her throat.

Diff and Holly scooted to the side to make room for the communications clerk, but Sally pushed between them and sat in the center. She flipped open her steno pad and found a pencil stuck behind her ear to write a short message to Diff. 'We both have pads, right?' she wrote. 'I bet we have a lot of other similar interests, right?' the note continued.

Before Diff could scrawl a reply, Holly took the pad and pencil from him to write a single word answer, 'WRONG!!!'

The sheriff stuck his finger in the fish tank's water and tasted the tip of his pinkie. "Well, it isn't booze," he announced to laughter.

"Holly dives well," Toms said with a puff on his pipe. "Maybe she should climb on the roof and do a swan dive into the tank. I saw that done in a carnival once a long time ago."

"That's a great idea," Sally chirped. "Maybe she should wear a necklace of heavy rocks so she can stay down longer."

Sheriff Downs's patience gave out as he said, "Let's get this show on the road." He called to the back room, "Ralph. Ralph Macon, you out there?"

Ralph called back, "Be with you in a sec. I'm getting my stuff together now."

"Hurry it up," Sheriff Downs said. "My office is running a traffic checkpoint today, and we need every man out there."

"I'm ready," Ralph said as he came into the room carrying a large model of a floatplane. "I think I've worked out something that will be of interest to all you men who are working on the case of my murdered partner."

"What about us women working on the case?" Sally muttered under her breath.

For the first time in a long while, Holly agreed with something Sally had said.

"We didn't come out here to watch you play with toys," Downs said as he started for the door. "Come on," he called to his deputies.

The men from the sheriff's department started to leave the room until Ralph called after them, "What's the greatest mystery you guys got in this case?"

Ray Wilson answered the question. "How my daughter and Diff saw a plane go down one day, and the same plane mysteriously appears two days later."

"That's what I thought," Ralph said. "So I called the company who made the floatplane and asked for an exact scale model. I've worked out the problem and have it set up in the tank to explain your mystery."

The sheriff, who had his hand on the front door, stopped and turned with interest. "I'm all ears, Ralph, but snap it up."

"Right, Sheriff," Ralph answered as he held the model over his head as if it were flying.

"If you go 'zoom, zoom, zoom,' I'm out of here," Downs said.

Ralph smiled, "Okay, no sound effects. The floatplane was flying above Loon Lake when Diff and Holly saw it smoke, wobble, and loose altitude." He brought the model down toward the fish tank. "Diff and Holly saw it crash in the water."

"That's what they say they saw," Ray said, "but a good search by police divers couldn't find the thing."

"I can't explain that," Ralph said, "except that the lake is deep and the water is dark down there. They must have just missed it."

"That still doesn't explain how it came to the surface two days later when we found the thing floating peacefully on the surface of the lake," Sheriff Downs said.

Ralph pushed the model into the water in a nose-down position. "Now follow me as I show how the plane hit the water. It was a powered crash, which means that the engine was still going and it was probably traveling at a pretty good clip when it hit the surface."

"We grant you that," Ray said, "but you still haven't solved anything here."

"Watch me." Ralph pushed the model plane under the water until its front was buried in the sand at the bottom of the tank. "She went straight in, and during the crash her front end took a terrible beating."

"Are you trying to say that tore the engine off?" Sergeant Toms said. "When we found her, she had lost her front end."

"Exactly!" Ralph said. "I wondered about that and a lot of other things until I finally figured it out. The engine mountings were weakened in the crash. It's probably a defect in the construction of this particular plane. It did have a powerful engine, perhaps a little too powerful for its general use. Because of its weight, the crash caused metal defects to appear which finally gave away and the engine fell off."

Sheriff Downs pointed a finger toward Ralph. "That does not compute," he said. "Plane crashes in water, plane's engine falls off, and the next thing you are going to say is that the loss of all that front-end weight allowed the pontoons to pull the plane back to the surface where we found it."

"That's exactly what I say," Ralph said.

"Well, I was out there on Loon Lake that day," Downs continued, "and no airplane popped to the surface like you say. If the engine fell off, it should have come up. . . ."

Ralph Macon shook his head. "You aren't listening to me, Sheriff Downs. The crash weakened the engine mountings, but it took time for them to work loose. When they finally did and the engine separated from the plane, the thing was lighter than the water and popped to the surface. . . . And that was two days later."

"Makes sense to me," Sergeant Toms said. Since this police officer did not often speak, what he said was usually well thought-out and respected. Everyone in the room also knew that Toms led the dive team that had searched for the plane that day.

"Then you admit that it's possible your men missed the plane during the search?" Ray asked.

"Anything is possible, Chief. I can say that this is the first explanation of the plane accident that I've heard that makes any sense. Since I do not believe in miracles, what Ralph has just said must have been how it happened. I don't know how we missed the wreckage on our search, but we obviously did."

"I wanted to be of some help, so I rest my case," Ralph said as he sat down.

Diff quickly wrote a note which he passed to Holly.

"Diff would like to know a few things," Holly said. "When you called the Mayday to this airport while we were over the lake, who did you speak with?"

"Gary, of course," Ralph answered. "He was the one on the radio who took my call and who called for the emergency rescue teams."

"True," Toms added. "I've heard the police recording of his 911 and it did sound like Gary."

Diff thought it was interesting that Ralph was flying the plane with him during the crash while Gary took the radio message. That seemed to leave few suspects if you didn't count the bank teller. Harry Black of Scenic Tours was beginning to head the shortlist of possible killers.

"Diff has another question," Holly said. "What happens to this business on your partner's death?"

"I now own all of it," Ralph answered.

"What about the dead man's wife?" Holly asked.

"The way we set it up, the partner who lived got the whole business. We had a large term insurance policy to pay off the dead partner's family. Believe me, Mary Acorn is well taken care of."

A sheriff's deputy stuck his head in the door, "There's something out here that you guys ought to see," he said. "I mean, talk about weird, this is it."

In the rush from the room, Sally stuck her foot out to trip Holly, but it was the gigantic Sheriff Downs who went down. He slid headlong across the floor to bang his head against the far wall. His deputies helped the enraged man to his feet. "Who did that?! I want to know who tripped me, because whoever did it is going to swing from the gallows!"

"We don't usually swing someone without some sort of trial first," Ray said as he tried not to laugh.

"I saw who did it," Sally said. "It's Holly's usual practical joke."

"Everybody out!" Chief Wilson bellowed to protect his daughter from the angry sheriff.

They lined up along the edge of the runway by the side of the Mountain Tours Piper Aztec. Just below the lettering "Mountain Tours" were scrawled red letters that read "Sweet Revenge!"

When Holly ran a finger along the edge of the first letter she said, "This paint is still wet."

"Who did this?" the sheriff bellowed at the deputy who had alerted them to the message.

"I didn't see who did it," the deputy replied.

"I wouldn't be surprised if our friend at Scenic Tours had something to do with this," Ray said as he signaled to Diff. Both men stalked toward the Scenic Tours offices next door.

The building seemed empty but Diff heard the sounds of running water and threw open the men's-room door. Harry Black was scrubbing red paint from his hands.

They looked at the swirling water in the sink with its distinctive red coloring. "That's very interesting stuff on your hands, Harry," Ray said. "Doing a little finger painting around here?"

"I had to retouch my plane today and spilled some paint," the nervous owner of Scenic Tours said rapidly. "Ralph is doing a number on me, isn't he? I knew he was up to something with that damn demonstration he put on. Am I supposed to be the one who crashed that thing and killed Mead?"

"How did you know about the demo?" Ray asked.

"Couldn't help but be curious when I saw all those cop cars parked in my front yard. Now leave me alone. I have lots of work to do."

"Did you splash paint on that plane?" Ray asked.

"I'm not answering without a lawyer," Harry Black said.

"I think you did and I think we had better have a little talk down at my office, Harry."

"Ralph is framing me, I know it," Harry said. He slammed the men's-room door and locked Diff and Ray outside.

"Help me break it in, Diff," Ray said as he slammed his shoulder against the door frame. The men threw themselves against the door until it splintered open on an empty room. The window was open. They looked out to see Harry run to a small MG sports car, jump inside, and race for the highway.

"Stop that car!" Ray Wilson bellowed until the cry was taken up by the sheriff, who yelled the same order to his men.

Within seconds three cars were racing after the convertible—two county sheriff cars and Diff James in a Morgan police cruiser. Diff had jumped through the window which put him the nearest to a cruiser. He pressed the gas to the floor as he followed the speeding roadster around the corner of the airport drive onto the highway.

Harry Black peered into his rearview mirror and saw the line of cars on his tail. The MG rocketed ahead as he floorboarded the gas.

Diff downshifted the cruiser to give it a boost and then slammed into high as he pressed the pedal to the floor. The snappy sports car was a pretty thing, but its engine was no match for the heavy-duty eight in the police cars. Gradually the law enforcement vehicles were gaining on the MG.

Harry braked and downshifted to spin his car in a bootlegger's turn. As his rear wheels locked, the car rocked back and forth before it skidded in a 180-degree turn that pointed it back in the opposite direction.

Diff decided against a U-turn and took a right turn on two wheels that skidded him down Main Street toward Bald Mountain Road. The sheriff's cars made U-turns, which put them even farther behind Harry Black and his roadster. The distance between the MG and sheriff's cars was gradually increasing.

Diff made another right on Bald Mountain Road and after two miles reached the highway intersection. He knew that the MG's route led back in this direction, so he was now ahead of the roadster. He pulled the car into the center of the highway and turned sideways to block both lanes.

The MG appeared in the distance with a string of sheriff's cars trailing far behind.

When he saw the blocking cruiser, Harry's first impulse was to brake. His car went into a skid that slid toward the parked cruiser. Diff took cover behind the car and waited. Harry changed his mind at the last minute and fought the wheel to turn back down the highway. He made a hard right to go around the cruiser, but his wheels hit a drainage ditch and the car flipped on its side with its wheels still turning.

Diff raced to the sports car and leaned into the driver's compartment to unbuckle Harry's seat belt. He levered the unconscious man over his shoulder and raced for the protection of the parked cruiser. He lay Harry on the pavement as the sports car exploded with a roar.

CHAPTER
10

Ray Wilson finished the phone conversation and put the receiver back on its cradle before he looked up at Diff and Holly sitting across his desk. "That was the hospital. They say that Harry Black has only minor injuries and will be released in two days." He tented his fingers. "I've been a cop for a lot of years," he said, "but this is the most confusing murder I have ever had."

"We haven't had many disappearing airplane cases since I can remember," Holly answered.

"Very funny," her father replied.

"Your killer's in the hospital right now, Daddy. Why don't you arrest Harry Black since he's the one who painted 'Revenge' on the murder plane? Then, to prove how guilty he is, he tried to run for it. He doesn't have any alibi for either time the murder could have taken place. He keeps telling everyone how Mountain Tours was trying to ruin him, which gives him motive."

Ray sighed and said, "Lots of people seem to have motives including the airport manager having an affair with the dead man's wife. Since you guys found it, need I remind you that Gary's truck had clay on it from the river near the Bean farm? You also found a machine-gun shell in his hangar."

Diff wrote a single-word note and gave it to the chief.

"Watson," Ray read. "Our henpecked bank teller does happen to be the only one in this case who has confessed. In fact, he called me this morning and confessed again."

It was time for Diff to write a longer note.

"You have a point, Diff," Ray said after reading it. "I'm not prepared to rule out Ralph Macon either. That was a convincing demonstration he put on for us with the model plane in the water tank, but I'm still not sure that's the way it happened. What all this means is that I'm in a corner here, because I have to make an arrest soon. And I mean very soon, or it's going to be my head. One of the things that still has to be checked out is Ralph Macon's alibi."

"He was piloting Diff and me when we saw the plane go down," Holly said.

"That's an ironclad alibi if that's when the murder took place. But to tie up all the loose ends, we have to know if Ralph was in New York from then until we found the plane."

"You want us to go to New York and find out?"

"You've got it," Ray said. "I asked Sally to make hotel reservations, so let me see how she did. Can you leave right away?"

"As soon as we throw a few things in a suitcase," Holly said as her father left the office to talk to Sally down the hall.

"Did you make separate room reservations?" Ray asked.

"How about separate hotels?" they heard Sally say. "You know, Chief, you really are a trusting guy. I was thinking of putting your daughter in a motel in New Jersey for her protection."

"Knock it off," they heard Ray say. Holly put her hands over her mouth to keep from laughing. "You know, Sally, the way you carry on I almost think you have a thing for Diff yourself."

"Oh, my God!" Sally said in a loud voice. "I wouldn't touch that freak with a ten-foot pole."

Holly's hands dropped as she looked at Diff's stricken face. She saw the passing waves of pain and knew he'd heard this sort of remark before. No matter how many times you heard an unkind thing, it was impossible not to feel hurt each time it happened. She took his hand and started toward the door. "Let's get going," she said. "We have a long drive to the city."

*   *   *

Diff drove the Saturn seventy miles per hour down the two-lane highway that led to the New York State Thruway. Although the Interstate would take them to the city, if Diff didn't slow down, Holly wondered if they'd make it alive.

She put her hand on his arm. "Take it easy, please. I know what you heard hurts, but Sally's angry and doesn't mean it." She saw a small muscle in his cheek begin to throb and wished there were something she could say or do to help him. She knew that at times like this he retreated into his most inner self.

Holly turned on the radio in the hope she could find some good jazz. Without good music, it was going to be a long and silent drive into the city.

When they turned off the West Side Highway to midtown New York, they entered a far different world than the quiet streets of Morgan. Crosstown traffic was bumper-to-bumper, and the city seemed to be all sound: honking taxis, screaming sirens in the distance, while crowded streets and sidewalks created sounds of their own.

Diff tried to make a turn on Eighth Avenue and cut off a delivery truck. The driver pulled even with the Saturn and leaned out his window. "What's the matter with you, dummy? Can't you drive?"

Diff's hands clenched the steering wheel as he stared straight ahead without looking at the yelling truck driver. When the light changed, they pulled away from the delivery truck with its screaming driver.

It was his slightly confused look that made Holly realize that this was Diff's first trip to New York City. She was traveling with a man who could rescue her from a strafing airplane and yet be thrown completely off balance by the traffic and noise of this huge city.

A cop leaned out the window of a police cruiser. "You are going the wrong way on a one-way street, buddy. I'd ticket you if we weren't going off duty. . . . You hear me? Answer me or you're buying trouble!"

Diff stared ahead without turning to look at the angry cop. "He can't talk!" Holly yelled across to the police.

"Tell him to take the turn now and get off the street!" the cop said as they drove off.

Diff made a turn into a bus stop and stopped the car. He got out and started walking up the street.

"Uh-oh," Holly said aloud. She knew that no matter how this man knew his way around forests, he was like a child in the ways of large cities. She slid across the seat to drive the car alongside Diff as he walked along the sidewalk. "Get in," she yelled over to him.

Diff shook his head and pointed to a large sign that

read, "Park Here." He folded his arms and leaned against a wall to wait.

Holly drove in the parking lot and turned the car over to the attendant. She grabbed their suitcases and said, "It's eight blocks to our hotel."

Diff picked up both suitcases and walked on as she hurried to catch up.

*   *   *

They had to wait half an hour in a reception room at the office of the airline before they were ushered into a vice president's office. The man they had come to see stood by his long mahogany desk. He wore an expensive suit and Italian shoes and seemed topped with a bald head that looked waxed. When he spoke it was in a pleasant, but slightly impatient voice.

"We have been asked by the Morgan police to talk with you about Mr. Macon," Holly said.

The vice president looked at the contents of a folder clamped between his hands. "I would guess that when you say the Morgan police, you mean your father," he said.

"Yes, that's true," Holly said, "but we're here to—"

"I know why you're here," the airline officer said quickly. "You are going to ask me about Ralph Macon and his contract."

"Yes, sir," Holly replied.

"We have investigated Mountain Tours very thoroughly and find them to be reliable and honest. It is unfortunate that one of the owners recently died."

"He was murdered," Holly corrected.

"That sort of thing seems to happen in the times we live in. We have been told and I am convinced that Mr. Macon can carry on without his partner."

"Yes, I'm sure he can."

"The contracts are signed, if that's what you came here to find out."

"Can you tell us when Mr. Macon signed his part of the contracts?" Holly asked.

The vice president flipped through another file folder before he answered, "It was signed on the 24th."

Diff knew that the 24th was the day the plane was discovered floating on Loon Lake. There was no way that Ralph Macon could have signed those contracts that day and also have killed his partner before the plane was discovered. Since he was piloting the plane with Diff when the floatplane crashed, he could not have killed his partner then either. It would seem that Ralph Macon could be removed from their list of suspects.

Holly had the same thoughts. She stood up and held out her hand to the vice president. "Thank you, sir, you have answered our question and we appreciate the time you gave us."

For the first time the vice president smiled as he walked them across his large office to the door. "It's been my pleasure. Actually, Mr. Macon was very thoughtful to keep us in phone contact when he faxed the signed contracts to us."

Diff stopped stock-still at the door and wrote a note, which he gave to the vice president: 'Is that legal?'

"It certainly is as long as we are certain that the proper person signed the contract as represented. We were on the phone with him that day and know that Mr. Macon actually signed the contract as we talked."

"Where was he calling from?" Holly asked.

"A little town called Waycross, which I believe is not far from Morgan. He said he needed to recruit another pilot for the program."

Back at their hotel over dinner, Diff wrote to Holly, 'Waycross is not a long drive from Morgan and it's even closer by airplane. Half of Macon's alibi has disappeared.'

Holly read the note twice and looked thoughtful. "We saw that plane smoke before it went into the water. Ralph was in the plane with us at that time, so we're his alibi and he doesn't need another one."

He replied by writing, 'Maybe that does cover him, but if we were somehow tricked, the plane could have been flown to the lake at a later time."

"No way, that's impossible," Holly said. "I know what we saw."

'I'm also curious as to why he was in Waycross when he told us he was in New York City. Let's go to Waycross first thing in the morning. It's a good excuse to get us out of this city. I'm a woods guy and here I'm like a fish flipping around on the ground after he's been hooked.'

I wish I had you hooked, Holly thought.

*   *   *

Waycross was a very old town. During the Revolutionary War it had been a fort on the Indian frontier, had been attacked several times, and had finally burned to the ground. The town had been rebuilt, but it had never regained its importance. Now it was a sleepy town on the edge of the forests and mountains of the Adirondacks.

Holly drove out of the city and up the New York State Thruway to the turnoff to Waycross. The nearer they got to town, the more nervous Diff seemed to become. In the early part of the trip, he just seemed glad to get away from the large city, but his nervousness increased as they approached the town where he was born.

His manner became even more tense when they came to the dirt road that went to what once had been the Dawkins farm. He reached over to pound on the horn and point at the dirt road leading to the farm.

"You want to go there?" she asked in amazement.

He nodded.

"You know how it hurts and you remember what memories it brings back?" She saw how determined he was and turned the car into the dirt road. They drove four miles over a weed-choked trace of a road that led back to the isolated Dawkins farm.

Nothing had changed since their last visit except that perhaps it was in a little worse condition because of the hard winter. The buildings were slowly falling apart. The house windows were broken, while the front door hung at an angle by one hinge. Rusted farm machinery seemed to sprout over the rear yard between house and barn.

"Do you really want to go in that place again?" she asked.

He didn't answer but continued to stare ahead as she drove around the farmhouse and stopped in the rear by the barn. Diff left the car and walked slowly to the barn doors, where he paused a moment before he went inside. Holly left him alone for a few minutes before she followed him.

He stood at the far end of the barn, staring into a wide hole in the floor that was the entrance to his childhood prison. In that place under the barn floor he had lived for many years.

They had finally discovered who Diff was and where he had come from less than a year ago. They had found this farm and the barn where he had been put after his mother died. His father, broken in will after the death of his wife, had in a sick way come to believe that his son was a monster that must be kept from sight.

The young boy had lived through much of his childhood and early adolescence as a prisoner under this barn's floor. His father tossed him scraps of food and forced him to live like an animal. Finally Diff dug a tunnel from the basement room to the outside on the far side of the barn. At night under the moon, he ran free in the woods, becoming like the animals of the night that he soon learned to imitate.

The mental abuse caused the young boy to grow into a young man who could not speak. Finally his father's heart attack had allowed him to escape. He had wandered dazed and confused through the woods until he reached Morgan, where he was helped by Ray Wilson.

Diff turned away from the hole in the floor and walked back to the car. Holly knew that in order to come to terms with himself, he must occasionally return to this place of hurt. It was necessary to relive those terrible times in order to try and reach an understanding of what his father had done to him.

"Where to now?" she asked as cheerily as she could when they were both back in the car.

'Let's try talking to the people at the local airport since they might be the ones to know about Ralph Macon,' he wrote.

"Gotcha," Holly said as she did a U-turn in the yard and drove back to the highway.

The Waycross Airport was a twin of the Morgan Airport. It contained a single runway with a few private planes parked along its edge. There was a low building for the airport offices and one hangar for repairs.

When they asked for the manager, they were directed to a back room where a tall woman of Holly's age was talking into a radio mike. An attractive brunette with hair cut in a very short pageboy, she was looking out the window that overlooked the runway. "Okay, Piper One Two Zero Niner, this is Waycross. Our runway runs north to south with a ten-mile-an-hour wind from the west. Visual flight rules are in effect and you are cleared for landing. Acknowledge. Over."

"Thankee, Waycross," a Texas drawl answered over the radio speaker on the wall. "ETA is five minutes from now. Over and out."

"ETA?" Holly asked.

"Estimated time of arrival," the airport manager answered as she replaced the mike on the radio. A name tag on her blouse told the world she was Kim Nobel. "What can I do for you two?"

"Do you know Ralph Macon from Morgan? He runs—"

"I know Ralph," was the quick answer. "Who in the flying business in this part of the state doesn't know him? He's pulled off quite a deal pairing Mountain Tours to that big airline."

"Have you seen him recently?" Holly asked.

"Sure, just the other day he flew in here on the—let me see." She flipped a calendar on the desk in front of the radio. "Yeah, Ralph came in on the 24th. I remember it distinctly because he asked to use my phone and fax machine."

"You know him pretty well, then?" Holly asked.

The woman's open manner seemed to cloud as she thought about the question. "What do you mean by 'pretty well'?"

"Like, how long have you known him?" Holly asked.

"Couple of years, I guess. As soon as I took over as manager, he flew over from Morgan for a social call. We went to dinner and . . . hey, what business is this of yours?"

"Police business," Holly said. "In other words, you two are dating?"

"From time to time. Listen, I may as well be frank with you. I am an employee here and not the owner. Ralph has asked me to fly for his new charter service and I have accepted. With his partner dead he needs another pilot, which is why he came to see me that day."

Diff handed Holly a note that she read aloud, "Are you a qualified flight instructor?"

"Yes, as a matter of fact, I am," Kim answered.

"Did you give flying lessons to Mary Acorn, the dead man's wife?"

"Sure did. She didn't want to take lessons from her husband or anyone in Morgan because she said it was going to be a surprise for her husband when she got her pilot's license."

"Did she get it?" Holly pressed.

"Sure did. Mary Acorn is one of the best natural pilots I've ever seen," Kim said.

CHAPTER 11

Diff drove the Saturn with one hand with his elbow resting on the open window. The drive from Waycross to Morgan was a pretty ride. A full moon gave the night ribbons of golden colors and he noticed how it glinted in Holly's red hair.

"Boy, isn't this a whole mess?" Holly said with a short laugh. "So Mary Acorn secretly learned to fly, which means that she didn't need Gary to help her kill her husband after all. She was completely capable of doing the deed herself."

As long as he was driving Diff couldn't answer by writing a note. He did wonder how Mary crashed the plane with her husband's body in it and still managed to escape the wreck.

"There's something else I wonder about," Holly said, "and that's the chemistry between Kim Nobel and Ralph. I have the feeling he flew to Waycross to do more than offer her a job. He could have done that over the telephone, which leads me to believe that they're involved."

Diff looked at her quizzically.

"I guess that look means you want to know how I know?"

He agreed with that.

"Women just know certain things like that. One clue was in a little bit of her body language when she spoke of him. . . . Miss Kim is more than half in love with Ralph."

When they neared the outskirts of Morgan, the Laman brothers' pickup was parked in front of the Morgan Bar as it often was.

"Passing that place makes me realize that we haven't had any dinner tonight and I am dying of thirst. Stop at the 7-Eleven, will you? Right now I could really munch one of their hot dogs along with a Coke."

The parking lot was empty, so Diff was able to park next to the front door. They found the lights on inside but no one at the counter. "I know he's here," Holly said. "If it's after banking hours, Henry is always here to closing, which means he's probably in the back room."

Diff got two hot dogs out of the grill and piled mustard and relish on their rolls. Holly drew two soft drinks and set them on the counter near the cash register. "I'm starved," she said as she took one of the hot dogs from Diff and ate a third of it in one bite. Two more bites finished the dog off, and she wiped her hands on a paper napkin. "I've got to pay for it since I've already eaten it. I wonder where he is?" When she looked at Diff, a worry line appeared on her brow. "My dad always has his men check on people in stores who work alone at night because places like this are an easy hit for a holdup."

Diff slapped his hot dog in her hand and ran for the back room. When the door handle wouldn't turn, he realized it was locked from the inside. He pounded on the door while

Holly called out, "Henry! Henry Watson, are you in there?"

Diff put his ear against the door and thought he heard a gasping sound that might be the sounds a man would make if he were bound and gagged. He stepped back and then ran forward to smash his shoulder against the flimsy door until it burst open under his attack.

A man's legs slowly swung back and forth in front of him. They heard more gasping sounds.

Diff grabbed a straight chair from the corner of the narrow storeroom and stood on it to lift up the small man's body on his shoulders. He opened his pocketknife to cut the rope that circled Henry Watson's neck.

Holly helped him lower the body to the floor. Henry's tongue stuck out and his eyes were bloodshot. When they took the rope off his neck, his breathing came in short wheezes and gasps.

"Thank God, he's still alive," Holly said.

"Why . . . why did you?" Henry's voice was hard to hear and understand as he struggled to speak. "Why? Why did you cut me down?"

"You tried to kill yourself, didn't you, Mr. Watson?" Holly asked.

"Yes," he gasped. As his breathing began to return to normal, he sat up to rub his neck. "Yes, I tried to. They wouldn't arrest me for the murder, you know? If I couldn't go to jail, what else could I do to get away from this place? She's got me working twenty hours a day, seven days a week. I can't stand it. I fell asleep at the bank today while taking care of a customer. I know I'm going to make a terrible error and give someone a thousand dollars for a ten-dollar check. I just want to die."

"You didn't kill Mead, did you?" Holly asked.

"Of course I didn't. I can't seem to kill anyone, including myself."

Holly walked over to the phone behind the counter. "I'm calling for an ambulance, Mr. Watson. I think that, for the time being, you've gotten yourself out of this store."

*   *   *

Ralph Macon leaned back in his desk chair and puffed on a long cigar. He blew rings toward the ceiling while his face broke into a wide grin. "It's looking good, huh, guys?" he asked Diff and Holly as they stood by the window of the Mountain Tours building watching the activity outside.

There were construction company trucks parked in front of the building. Diff saw that a cellar had been dug and cement blocks had been laid to enclose it. Workmen were flooring the room and raising the walls for an enlarged waiting room.

"Yep," Ralph continued with a self-satisfied grin. "The bank couldn't wait to loan me all sorts of money when they saw my contract with the airlines. We're rebuilding this place by adding on a real fancy waiting room and restaurant. The insurance company is paying off on the floatplane and I have a new pontoon jobber ordered, plus two more Piper Aztecs. Yes, sir, Mountain Tours is in business . . . real business."

"I guess that's why you need Kim Nobel as another pilot?" Holly asked.

"Not only Kim, but two other pilots are coming on board. This little outfit is going to really grow. You know, we could have done this long ago if old Mead wasn't such a pussycat. He was always afraid to expand and said a small sky-tour company was just right for him. Keeping it small meant fewer worries and less work. He didn't want to work very hard and wanted plenty of time off for fishing. You know, he'd sometimes fly fishermen into the camp at Lake Walpie and wouldn't fly out again for four days. He'd just stay on and fish right along with our customers and leave all the other work for me. To tell you the truth, guys, I guess I'm better off without him. Not that I want to see anyone check out with a bullet in the back of his head, but . . . it's an ill wind that doesn't blow someone some good."

"Are you and Kim Nobel lovers?" Holly asked.

"None of your business," Ralph answered without losing his self-satisfied look. "She called me last night and said you two were sucking around trying to get info on me."

"I think you've answered our question," Holly said.

When Ralph stubbed out his cigar, his grin faded to a glare. "You know something, you two are becoming quite unpopular around these parts. You're evidently leaning on Gary and Mary Acorn, while poor Harry Black is going ape over this stuff. Everyone in town knows that Henry Watson is so screwed up over this case that he's in the psycho ward at Morgan Hospital. Way to go, guys. Worst day's work I ever did was to give you two a free airplane ride."

'That free ride is going to save your neck,' Diff wrote in the note he gave to Ralph.

"What's that supposed to mean?" Ralph snapped.

"It means that the airline people say you faxed the contract to them and weren't in New York City on the 24th," Holly said. "Your alibi for that day is gone, shot, kaput, nixed; so you had better be glad you had us with you the day the plane went down."

Ralph's attitude changed. "You make a good point. All right, I'm sorry I lit into you, but I lost my temper. Maybe I got to be nice to you guys since you are my alibi."

"If what we saw that day was true, then you're okay," Holly said.

"True? Of course it's true. We all saw Mead's plane go into the drink."

"Maybe," Holly answered.

"We saw him crash on Loon Lake," Ralph insisted. "I proved with the model how the engine came off later, which allowed the plane to come to the surface. Mead was killed that day and dropped in the water."

"Who was flying the plane and how did he get away?" Holly asked.

Ralph shrugged. "How do I know? I'm not a cop. Maybe the killer had SCUBA gear in the cockpit and swam underwater to a far part of the lake before he came to the surface. I don't know exactly what happened, but I do know we saw that plane go down when we three were together."

*   *   *

Diff stood on the shore of Loon Lake and looked out over the water. He heard Holly behind him setting out their picnic on the table under the trees. When he awoke that morning he had looked out his window toward the big house. The lights had been on in the kitchen, and he could see Holly working at the stove as she prepared a fancy picnic lunch for them.

He had smiled at her in the distance and wished he were in the kitchen with her. He could imagine sitting at the table watching her cook eggs and bacon. Perhaps he would go up behind her and put his arms around her waist and nuzzle the back of her neck. She would turn in his arms and smile before they kissed.

He dropped his robe and jumped into a cool shower that made him yip as he shivered under the cold water. It might be an old wives' tale, but cold showers did work.

"Lunch in two and a half minutes," Holly said from the picnic table.

"Right, honey. I know it's going to be great," is what he wanted to say but couldn't. In fact, he couldn't talk about the weather, much less tell her how he felt about her. He opened his mouth to speak and no sound came. He felt himself suddenly carried back in time until he was surrounded by the musty smell of the hole under the barn floor. He was a small child again who cried into the burlap sacks that were his bedding until his whimpering stopped as all his words and cries disappeared.

He willed himself back to the present and this place. He was standing on the bank of Loon Lake looking toward where an airplane had crashed and a dead man had been discovered. He would think of those things and not of the speech he could not make to the woman behind him whom he could not hold.

Once again he was able to see the floatplane as they flew over the lake with Ralph at the controls. Smoke poured from the engine as the pilot fought for control.

Mead Acorn had been shot once in the back of the head. He was not able to fly anywhere after the bullet had killed him instantly. Someone in the seat next to him had flown that plane until something went wrong with the engine and the plane crashed.

Possibly the killer had intended to fly to one of the lakes beyond Bald Mountain. At some deserted spot he might hide the body in the woods where it would never be found.

Had the killer been caught by surprise when the smoking engine failed? If so, what happened to the pilot at the controls of the plane? Mead was already dead, but the pilot might have gotten the door open and gotten out of the plane as it sank.

They did not see anyone come to the surface. If the killer died in the crash, why wasn't his body in the plane when it came to the surface? Had the murderer forced the door and gotten out of the plane but then drowned?

After a drowning, body gases cause it to come to the surface after three days unless it is weighted down. No other body had come to the surface of Loon Lake.

"Lunch," Holly announced.

Diff turned away from the lake wondering what had happened out there on the day of the murder.

He stood at the picnic table and admired the meal Holly had prepared. She had spread a colorful tablecloth over the picnic table and covered it with the contents of the wicker basket: deviled eggs, pickles, olives, and celery stuffed with cheese, along with cooked shrimp and sauce. There seemed to be half a dozen different types of sandwiches, each one fancier than the last. Iced tea brimming with ice and a lemon slice was cool and tall. Fat chocolate-chip cookies were dessert.

"Like it?" she asked.

All he could do was shake his head in wonder and hope he didn't get too fat.

CHAPTER 12

Sally was the first arrival for the meeting at the chief's house. She sat stiffly in a straight chair in front of the table with her steno pad arranged neatly in front of her. She looked like a disapproving schoolteacher, or perhaps a cop watching a jaywalker. The angry young woman glared at Holly, who was the only other person in the room. "Where's your lover?" she asked.

"We are not lovers," Holly said.

"Sure, and I have two heads. Anyone who knows Diff can see the way he looks at you."

"He does?" Holly asked in true surprise.

"Well, continue to go ahead with what you're doing. It's no skin off me. Just realize that you are getting a very bad rep in this town. Why, if your dad wasn't chief of police, they'd probably ban you."

"Why do you go around all the time bad-mouthing me?"

107

Holly asked. "I don't say anything to other people that I don't say to your face."

Others began to arrive at the house. Holly knew them all well as they were the same group that had a brainstorming session earlier in the case. Her dad arrived riding with Sheriff Downs in his Mohawk County cruiser, while Sergeant Ned Toms came in a Morgan police car. Diff walked down the stairs of his apartment and across the drive.

"Everyone here?" Ray asked as he took charge of the meeting. "I really need all your help on this thing," he said. "*The Morgan News* is running stories that ask for my head. The mayor wants to meet with me this afternoon to find out if I've made an arrest yet. The question is, ladies and gentlemen, whom do I arrest?"

Sergeant Toms slowly lit his pipe and spoke in his usual calm manner. "Harry Black of Scenic Tours has motive but no alibi and painted 'Revenge' on the planes. Since he also took off and ran and we had to chase him, I think you've got your man, Chief."

"Mary Acorn had two motives: her love for Gary topped with a million in insurance money," Holly said. "Her guilt is proven by the fact that she took secret flying lessons."

Sheriff Downs looked unhappy. "I say we lean on Ralph Macon of Mountain Tours since he lied to us about going to the city and he benefits by the death of his partner. I'm suspicious over that business between him and that woman pilot from Waycross."

"That's all fine and dandy, Sheriff, except that Ralph was flying Diff and Holly when the floatplane crashed," Ray said. "He's the one who radioed the Mayday, which gives him a perfect alibi if you ask me."

The room was silent until Sally blurted out, "You want me to draw an arrest warrant for all of them, Chief?"

"Yep," Ray said.

"Yep who?" Sally pressed.

Diff scribbled a note for Holly.

"Diff writes, 'Arrest no one until tomorrow. Who's the killer will depend on exactly how the murder was done. Give me the rest of the day and tomorrow to put it together.'"

"You know something we don't?" Sheriff Downs asked.

Diff shook his head.

"I think what he means is that he'll find a solution before tonight," Holly said.

Why didn't I say that first? Sally thought. *That Holly is really man-smart and acts like a big cat who's going to eat her catch before he knows what caught him.*

"You have until six tomorrow," Ray said.

*　　*　　*

Diff paddled his canoe in a slow course across Loon Lake. There was no wind to ripple the water. The sky was a deep blue with a few puffs of white cloud that chugged lazily over him. He lifted the paddle from the water and let forward momentum carry him across the still lake.

He looked toward Bald Mountain and then turned to see the small dock at his rear. He estimated that he was nearly in the center of the lake near where they had seen the floatplane crash. They had watched the plane disappear without a trace only to find it on the surface two days later.

Diff did not believe in magic. He knew that nearly everything had a logical answer if you knew the science and thought about it long enough. There must be an answer here besides Ralph's theory. It was difficult to believe that the engine just happened to fall off and its release allowed the floatplane to rise to the surface.

He looked into the clear water as if it could show a

replay of the plane crash. All that he saw was the reflection of the woods and two moose standing in the shallows munching grass.

He looked up sharply at the moose. They were too far away to worry about him and continued eating. The smaller of the animals was farther out in the water than its mother. Diff let his gaze shift from the eating animals back to their reflection in the water.

A breeze blew from the mountain and rippled the surface of the lake, which turned the moose reflection into wavy lines. The mild breeze quickly passed and the water returned to normal. The moose still grazed on the tender water grass.

Diff could not take his eyes off the two large animals by the shore of the lake. They finished their meal and walked slowly into the woods.

An idea began to grow. The image of the distant animals combined with the memory of the crashing plane flowed together. He knew how the murder had taken place and this knowledge narrowed the list of suspects.

Diff turned the canoe to paddle as rapidly as he could toward the small dock at the edge of the Morgan Airport.

He ran the canoe ashore at the edge of the narrow beach near the dock. He jumped into knee-deep water to pull the canoe above the waterline before he ran for his pickup parked a few feet away.

There was another item to be checked out before he had Holly make a few phone calls.

He drove around the airport's runway and parked in front of the snack bar and office. He went around to the side of the building and looked in that window of the radio-office-control tower. Gary sat before the radio with his back to Diff. A tripod in front of the picture window that looked out over the runway held a powerful telescope.

It was pointed across the lake toward Bald Mountain.

When Ralph radioed the Mayday, the message had been taken by Gary. The airport manager with radio mike in one hand and his other hand on the telescope could have followed the activity over the lake. Another interesting item that narrowed the suspects.

Diff drove back to the house, lost in thoughts of the phone calls he was going to ask Holly to make for him.

The Saturn was not in the driveway, but a glance at his watch told him that her classes at the school for the deaf would soon be over. He took the stairs to his apartment three at a time.

He had to write Holly a long note with instructions for several phone calls. It would take far too long to write out his plan on a pad, so he switched on the computer and clicked into a word processing program.

Diff had just finished his long computer message when the Saturn turned in the drive. He waved out the window.

Holly smiled up at him as she started toward the garage apartment. He wondered what had happened in her day to make her so happy.

*   *   *

They gathered on the shore of Loon Lake. Morgan's police department was represented by all three of its cruisers, while Sheriff Downs arrived in his car followed by another full of deputies. The local newspaper had a reporter and photographer on hand. Someone had alerted the ambulance corps, and their emergency unit was parked by the shore. For some strange reason, the Morgan Fire Department hook-and-ladder truck was parked at the far end of the lot.

As the convoy of cars and trucks was seen driving toward the lake, curious townspeople followed in their cars and pickups.

A row of invited guests was standing between the two groups of police. Mary Acorn, wife of the dead man, stood next to Gary, who wore his usual flight jacket and Air Force cap. As usual, Harry Black of Scenic Tours glared at Ralph Macon of Mountain Tours.

Diff parked by the dock and carried a fishing-rod case over his shoulder as he walked out on the dock to the rowboat. Yesterday Holly had made the phone calls he had asked, and the requested materials had arrived by special messenger.

"We're ready when you are, Diff," Ray called.

Holly cast off the line and watched Diff row across the lake to the side where the moose often ate. When he was almost to his spot, she went to his pickup and climbed in the back to prepare her part of the reenactment.

A twin-engine Cessna taxied to the edge of the runway nearest the lake. Kim Nobel idled the engines as she leaned out the window to yell over to Ray. "Diff wants me to take you and Sheriff Downs for a plane ride, Chief."

"What's going on here?" the sheriff asked.

"You got me," Ray said as he climbed into the aircraft. "Let's do what the lady wants since it seems to be part of Diff's plan."

"I don't have time for a joyride while our mute friend goes fishing," Sheriff Downs said. "Look at him out there." He pointed to Diff at the far side of the lake who had stopped rowing and seemed to be sitting in the center of the boat holding a fishing pole.

"He's up to something," Ray said. "Diff wouldn't get us out here on a goose chase unless he had good reason."

The two senior police officers were so large that they had to wedge themselves deep in their seats to make room for each other before strapping themselves in.

Kim increased engine power and turned the plane down the runway. She began their takeoff roll and they were soon airborne. At a thousand feet she began a banked turn away from Morgan to head back toward the lake and the distant Bald Mountain.

Kim put on earphones with an attached throat mike. "This is Cessna One Oh One, Holly. Do you read me?" she said. She listened for a moment, and then said, "I read you five by five ground. We are now approaching Loon Lake and are ready when you are. . . . Yes, I'll tell my passengers." She turned to face Chief Wilson and Sheriff Downs. "That man out on the lake in the rowboat is going to show you exactly what happened the day Mead Acorn was killed."

"I'll believe that when I see it," the sheriff snorted. "I just wish he'd make it snappy because these seats are too small for men like Ray and me."

The pilot didn't pay any attention to the sheriff's remarks. Kim flew the plane on a straight course over Loon Lake directly in line with Bald Mountain. She picked up a clipboard that Diff had prepared. "We're going to do everything exactly like Diff and Holly did the day they saw the plane go down."

"Suits me," Ray said. "I suspect he's probably on to something."

"Sounds to me like we're playing games," the sheriff said.

"Hey!" Kim read from the clipboard. "Look at that plane down below us. It looks like Mead. My partner has taken the floatplane out for a test flight."

She nosed the plane down to give the two police officers a better view. In the distance in front of and below them and directly over the center of the lake was a bright-red, single-engine plane with pontoons. "Look at that baby go," Kim read from the clipboard the exact words that Ralph Macon had spoken the day Diff and Holly saw the crash.

"Hey, what's going on? He's in trouble," Kim read.

They watched a thin trail of black smoke trail from the plane below them. The craft seemed to be fighting to keep a straight course.

"Where in the hell did that thing come from?" Sheriff Downs asked.

"It's an exact duplicate of the plane that crashed," Ray said in disbelief.

"He's really in trouble," Kim read in a monotone. "He's in deep—"

The plane below them went into a steep dive.

"Hey!" the sheriff said in alarm. "It looks like he's going to go in!"

The plane wagged its wings as it sank toward the water. "She's going down," were the last words Kim read.

The two police officers watched in horror as the plane rammed into the surface of the lake and immediately sank.

"It's gone!" the sheriff nearly screamed. "The plane's gone in and your idiot friend is sitting in the boat not moving. He should row over to where the plane went in and try to save the pilot. He's still got that fishing rod in his hand. I'm going to bust him! I have never in my whole career seen such disregard for human life. He sat and watched a plane crash and never even stopped fishing."

CHAPTER
13

Sheriff Big Red Downs stood on the shore of Loon Lake and shook his fist at the rowboat. Diff calmly looked up.

"You're going to get busted over this!" the sheriff bellowed toward the rowboat before he turned to scream at his deputies. "Don't just stand there! Get a boat and go out to see if you can save the pilot of that plane. You heard me, get going!"

Diff took his fishing rod apart and slipped it back in its carrying case. He dipped the oars back in the water and began to row toward the dock. The angry sheriff continued to yell at him, "You get over to where that plane went down! You hear me? That's an order!"

Holly walked over to try and calm the angry man. "That won't be necessary, Sheriff."

"Stay out of this, young lady, and stop trying to protect your boyfriend from his rotten actions." The sheriff pulled his service revolver from its holster. "If he doesn't follow a police order, I might just give him a warning shot across his bow."

"Easy now," Ray said as he put his hand on the sheriff's arm. "I'm sure Diff will explain everything."

"He had better have a damn good explanation as to why he sat out there and didn't lift a finger to help a doomed pilot," the sheriff said.

Diff tied the boat to the dock and slung his fishing-pole case over his shoulder. He wrote in his pad as he walked toward them.

"No plane went down," Holly said. "Well, at least not a plane like you think."

"I know what I saw with my own eyes," the sheriff snapped. "Ray and I are trained observers who watched a red pontoon plane fly below us. Its engine started to smoke before it dove into the water and disappeared."

"That's exactly what Diff and I saw the other day. Then the divers couldn't find any wreckage until two days later when the plane magically came to the surface."

The sheriff scowled. "I don't believe in the tooth fairy, the Easter Bunny, Santy Claus, or little people who live under mushrooms. I know what I saw. As I told you, your dad and I are trained observers who have spent our lives looking for clues, investigating crimes, and sizing up suspects. That's what we do for a living, so I know darn well what I saw today."

Diff handed him a note.

"What do you mean it wasn't a real crash?" the sheriff mumbled.

Diff pointed at Holly.

"We can do it again," Holly said. "This time you'll see how it was done." As she ran back to the pickup, Diff took the fishing-pole case from his shoulder and unzipped the covering. He took out the rod and put it together before he threw a small switch attached to the handle. He pointed the pole over the lake while he turned a small lever mounted where the reel would ordinarily be.

They heard the start-up whine of a tiny aircraft engine from the bed of the pickup truck. A single-engine pontoon plane flew over the truck cab and across Loon Lake.

"That's a toy!" the sheriff thundered. "That's not what I saw. That's nothing but a kid's toy."

Diff shook his head as he continued operating the radio-controlled airplane from his fishing pole antenna. The small craft continued to the middle of the lake where smoke began to pour from its engine. It seemed to rock back and forth before going into a dive directly into the water where it disappeared.

"Now do you see how it was done?" Holly said as she rejoined them.

"No way," the sheriff said. "We saw a real airplane up there."

"No, sir," Holly said. "You thought you saw a full-size airplane because that's what you were told by the pilot. If you remember, you were flying above the pontoon plane as it flew below and ahead of you. In your range of vision you had no landmarks of known size between you and the pontoon plane. It was farther below you than you realized, which made you think you were seeing a real crash by a normal airplane."

"Then the killer operated a radio-controlled device that appeared to you two to be a real airplane?" Ray asked.

"Yes, the murderer fooled us the same way we demonstrated to you, although he wasn't out on the lake in a rowboat. It's an optical illusion that comes down to a question of perspective. You are told a certain thing is full size and you assume it is. What we all actually saw was an exact duplicate that was a scale model of the real floatplane."

The sheriff's anger began to fade as he realized that what they were telling him was more than possible. "Okay, I'm beginning to buy what you say, but where did you get those models?"

"From the same place the killer did," Holly said.

"Which is where?" the sheriff snapped.

"From the manufacturer of the pontoon plane."

Ray put it together first as his eyes scanned the crowd standing along the lakefront. "We saw a model plane like that once before," he said, "when Ralph gave us a demonstration of how the engine could have come off."

"Isn't it interesting," Holly said, "that Ralph bought several radio models a week before we saw the plane go down?"

The sheriff began to look confused. "If you two saw a model go into the drink like you just duplicated for us, what happened to the actual plane with the dead man in it?"

"Diff thinks that Ralph wanted us to see the plane crash in order to be his alibi witnesses," Holly said, "which is why we saw the plane go into the lake while we were piloted by Ralph Macon."

"Then he was able to control the radio model while he flew you?" Ray said.

"Yes," Holly answered. "He had the controls hidden by his side away from us when he operated it. What really happened is that he killed Mead early that morning and hid the floatplane. Two days later he flew the pontoon plane over the lake and glided to a silent landing just before dawn. He dropped the engine and left the plane on the lake for you to find."

"The plane was full of water when we got there," Downs said.

"Pumped in," Holly said.

Ray had been searching the crowd as Holly talked. "He's not here," he said. "Ralph was here a minute ago and now he's gone."

Both police officers began to shout directions to their men for an immediate search of the area. Town police and sheriff's department cruisers raced to the front and rear gates to block the exit roads so that no one could leave the vicinity of the lake and airport. Other police officers formed a line that moved slowly through the small crowd of spectators. In this small town, the police knew all the adults by sight and would quickly recognize Ralph Macon if he were here.

Holly noticed that the ambulance doors were closed although not too long ago she had seen Roy Jenkins sitting in the open door watching the activity. She pressed her ear against the side of the ambulance and heard low voices.

She waved to her father and pointed. Ray and Sergeant Toms moved quickly to the rear of the ambulance with drawn guns.

Half a dozen cops armed with revolvers and rifles surrounded the rear of the ambulance. Ray stepped forward and yanked open the rear doors.

"We've got you cov—" His voice died.

"Oh, my," Holly said. Locked in a tight embrace as they sat on the stretcher inside the ambulance were Roy Jenkins and Sally Way.

Holly laughed. It would seem that her competition with Sally over Diff had been solved. The communications clerk was obviously interested in someone else.

The search continued. Since the airport was surrounded by a high chain-link fence, patrol cars drove around the perimeter to stop anyone trying to climb over it. Officers at the two gates checked everyone who left. Another group of officers moved in a line across the runway toward the buildings near the entrance.

When the police and deputies reached the airport office, they drew guns and pressed against the outside wall before they rushed the door and took up firing positions inside the building. Room by room, alert cops with drawn guns continued the search.

Ray and Sheriff Downs followed their men and snapped orders to assign areas that might have been overlooked.

After they searched the airport office building, they went in the hangar, then the Mountain Tours building, and finally the Scenic Tours building.

Ralph had disappeared. He had seemingly not left the airport, but he could not be found inside the grounds.

Ray, Diff, and Holly walked over to where Red Downs was giving orders on his police radio. "I've set up roadblocks on all roads leaving Morgan and the county," he said. "Of course, he could hike cross-country and might slip through any search we can mount."

"I can't figure out how he got out of here without being seen," Ray said.

"I think he slipped away before the demonstration was finished," Downs said. "He knew the jig was up and did his disappearing act before we were on to him."

Ray looked grim. Diff and Holly knew the chief would search every inch of the airport and its buildings a second time, and when that was done, he would have it searched again. If Ralph Macon was anywhere on the grounds of the Morgan Airport, he would be found.

*　　*　　*

They called off the search at six that night. Ray was convinced that Ralph Macon had escaped from the area and by now was probably two hundred miles away. Tired cops holstered guns as they began to walk back to their cars to drive slowly through the gate.

"I'll see you at the house," Ray yelled over to Diff and Holly. "When you get home, whip up a salad and I'll throw steaks on the grill."

As they climbed into the pickup, Holly said, "I just remembered that we forgot lunch. No wonder I'm so starved."

Diff turned the ignition and the well-maintained truck engine purred to life. He drove slowly toward the front gate and noticed that they were last in the line of cars and trucks leaving the airport.

As they started past the Mountain Tours building he jammed on the truck's brakes. "What's the matter?" Holly asked. "Oh, that's Ralph's building, which has been searched at least four times. It's not a big place to begin with and there isn't any place to hide. I promise you, he's not in there, so let's go rustle up food."

Diff stepped out of the truck with the uneasy feeling that something had been overlooked at this building. He walked inside through the open door.

Even with the new waiting room Ralph had added, it was not a very large building. Diff had gone along with Sergeant Toms and two other men when they had searched this building for the third time.

Still, there was a tiny thought in the back of his mind that he could not quite catch. He walked through the rooms to see that all places large enough for a man to hide had been searched.

He stopped stock-still in the center of the new waiting room. As if in a dream, he vividly remembered the hole in the barn floor where his father had kept him prisoner during those horrible years. Why did this place at this time remind him of that personal prison? He paced the waiting room again and again.

"What are you thinking about, Diff?" Holly asked quietly from the doorway. "There's nothing here."

He remembered that the last time they talked to Ralph the carpenters had been working on this room which even now was not quite finished. The cellar had been dug, the flooring laid, and the walls were up. Now a roof enclosed the room, but the finishing work had not been done.

Where was the cellar door?

He walked outside to go completely around the building to make sure there was no cellar entrance. How could that be? He distinctly remembered the carpenters putting the flooring over an enclosed space under the waiting room floor. There had to be at least a large crawl space under that floor.

Viewed from the outside, it looked as if the building was constructed on a concrete slab. The foundation appeared to be at ground level, and yet Diff had seen space under the floor.

He walked back to the unfinished waiting room. The only doors to the room were ones to the office and closet, two to what would become restrooms, and the outside door.

Diff opened the door to the closet built in the corner and knelt down. The flooring had not been finished and was only plain plywood that would eventually be covered by tile or carpeting.

He reached down to find that one of the boards was loose. He worked the blade of his pocketknife along the edge until it tilted forward.

The false floor inside the closet was a trapdoor leading down to space below the building.

Ralph Macon waited for them with a .45 automatic pointed at their heads. "One move and I will blow you both apart," he said in a quiet voice. "Man, oh, man, I couldn't have planned this better if I'd thought a year. My prisoners are the guy who can't speak and the top cop's daughter. I think I see my way out of here, and you two are going to provide me with the transportation and a free ride."

"There's still a police guard at the gate," Holly said. "They'll search the truck as we leave."

"We shall see, my little lady, we shall see," Ralph said as he pointed the .45 at her. "At least you won't require a gag," he said to Diff.

"I've wanted to ask you two questions," Holly said. "What did you pay the Laman brothers for, and who wrote 'Revenge' on both planes?"

"Harry Black really did want revenge or at least wanted to scare us. I had the Laman boys do a number on his planes one night. He knew I had put them up to it and he retaliated. Nice fit, huh? Now, let's go."

The Piper Aztec had been pulled inside the airport hangar and the large outside doors shut. Ralph waved the .45 at Diff. "Climb into the plane, lover boy, and sit at the controls." He snatched the truck keys from Diff's pocket and replaced them with his own ring and watch. "Fair trade, huh?"

When Diff was seated in the pilot's seat, Ralph hit him on the side of the head with the pistol barrel and watched him slump over the control panel.

"What are you doing?" Holly cried in a frightened voice.

"You might think your boyfriend here is better-looking than me," Ralph said, "but did you ever notice that we are just about the same build?"

"I never thought about it," Holly said.

Ralph tied her in a chair not far from the tool chests. "Well, you and I are going to drive out of here in his truck," he said. "No police guard is going to stop the chief's daughter and her boyfriend."

"What about Diff?"

"Your friend here is going to take a little trip to hell in my place." He went behind the tool rack and rolled out a large drum of fuel. He filled a five-gallon can from the drum and carried it over to the plane. He uncapped the can and began to pour gasoline over Diff and the cabin.

"Why did you kill your partner?" Holly asked.

"He was content to be a plane jockey for the rest of his life. You notice that little hole where I hid? I've been wanting to build that for a couple of years. It's a foolproof place to hide illegal aliens and drugs. A good bush pilot like me can fly all sorts of interesting things over the border. Big ticket things that certain people will pay quite well to have me keep in the hole until they're ready."

Ralph finished sloshing gasoline around the plane cabin.

"What are you going to do?" Holly asked in alarm.

"In a couple of seconds your friend is going to become a Roman candle," Ralph said. "While he burns to a crisp, the reliable chief's daughter will rush out of here shouting for help, followed by her mute friend. When they finally put out the fire, the body will be unrecognizable but close enough in build to be me. You and I will take a one-way trip out of here, but don't worry, you won't be going far."

"Don't! Help, po—" Holly began to yell until her voice was muffled by the tape Ralph slapped across her mouth.

Diff began to moan and stir in his seat.

"Night-night time," Ralph said. He picked up an old newspaper from a tool bench and rolled it up before he lit the end with a cigarette lighter. When the paper was burning well, he walked toward the plane to throw the flaming torch at the spilled gasoline.

A large dark form hurtled through the air with a deep growl and struck Ralph in the chest. Knocked back by the weight of the huge dog's body, Ralph staggered and fell against the tool chest, which rolled over on the drum of high-octane gasoline.

The drum of fuel that spilled over Ralph burst into flames with an exploding whoosh! Fire immediately raged in the hangar.

Holly, tied to the chair, tried to hobble away from the flames but fell over on the floor.

Diff opened his eyes and shook his head to regain focus. The heat began to warm and cloud the room. Flames would soon reach the spilled gasoline that filled the plane cabin.

He staggered over to Holly. He tried to untie her, but

the pain of the blow and the approaching flames made him clumsy. He knew they had only seconds until his gasoline-soaked clothing ignited. He lifted the chair with Holly in it and stumbled from the hangar and across the runway until he fell gasping on the grass.

The burning airplane inside the hangar exploded with a roar.

Fire-engine and police sirens could be heard in the distance. Diff was finally able to untie Holly's hands, which she immediately used to cling to him.

Light from the burning hangar turned twilight into day as a very large dog limped through the smoke-filled doorway to come over and lick Diff's hand.